# FIGHTING OVER ME

ESPECIALLY FOR GIRLS™
presents

# FIGHTING OVER ME

## BY MARJORIE SHARMAT

Dell Publishing Company, Inc.

NEW YORK

This book is a presentation of Especially For Girls™, Weekly Reader Books.
Weekly Reader Books offers book clubs for children from preschool through high
school. For further information write to: **Weekly Reader Books,**
4343 Equity Drive, Columbus, Ohio 43228.

Especially For Girls™ is a trademark of Weekly Reader Books.

Edited for Weekly Reader Books and published by arrangement with
Dell Publishing Co., Inc.,
1 Dag Hammarskjold Plaza, New York, NY 10017.

Printed in the United States of America.

ISBN 0-440-92530-4

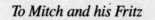

*To Mitch and his Fritz*

**N**obody expected much of me.

Nobody expected me to become spring queen of the entire Palm Canyon High School. Queen to Mitchell Brenner's king. And he's something else. He's looking at me in a new way now. Any way would be new, I guess, because he never looked at me at all before.

Nobody expected that he would have competition from another guy for me, that Seth Berns would come into my life and want to stay.

Nobody expected Chi Kappa Sorority, the exclusive ten-members-only sorority, to chase me to become a member. Especially since I already belonged to The Pack, the democratic sorority.

Nobody expected mysterious, menacing messages to arrive in my mailbox.

Nobody expected any of these shocking things to hap-

pen to me, Fritzi Tass, who reached her senior year of
high school without anyone's really noticing she was
there.

I must be the "nobody expected" girl.

But there was one exception. My parents used to
expect *everything* from me. We're talking top-of-the-
heap here. My mom and dad expected me to be an aca-
demic whiz. They both graduated from college, and they
kept telling me that graduating from college was "the
minimum" they expected from me. The maximum was
never put into words. I think they had something crazy in
mind like Fritzi Tass, college professor.

I wanted Fritzi Tass, commercial artist.

I also wanted to be this big towering social success in
school. Who doesn't? Being a social success is serious
business in high school. My big problem was that nobody
took me seriously. I had a social disease: I was chronically
enthusiastic. Perky. Eager. But you are what you are,
right?

I dated now and then, but of course none of the guys
took me seriously. Girls didn't either. None of them con-
fided in me.

Not that I exactly blamed them. I have this little weak-
ness, inherited from my mother who's the same way, for
spreading information. Okay, not necessarily information. Sometimes it was just gossip. Tell Fritzi Tass, tell the
world.

My mother's influence didn't stop there. She got dis-
gusted with my marks, so she started to do my homework
for me. "All you need is a little push to get you moving,"
she said as she took over ninety percent of my work. Some
of my teachers think I'm a *genius*. Some of them know

better. And all the kids know better. Listen, I never kept it a secret. I was proud of my mother's work. She was up there with the best of them.

So that's the way things stood, and I kept hoping that someday I'd at least get a big social break. I figured that the biggest would have been getting asked to join Chi Kappa Sorority. I mean, that's instant popularity. Since they only allow ten members, there has to be an opening to get in. Usually the openings happen when members graduate or move, but during the past few months two girls, Kim Adler and Tracy McVane, actually *quit!* Kim quit first. She was the first member ever to quit. It was plenty brave, quitting all that popularity. Rona Dunne's president of Chi Kappa, and she's the most popular girl in school. Another member, Carrie Reis, isn't far behind her, although Tracy managed to mess up some of Carrie's popularity before Tracy quit. Good thing too. Carrie deserved it.

Most of the members of Chi Kappa are kind of snobby, but they've got the power, and power gets you respect. I think that's absolutely the most disgusting thing about power. But instead of trying to do something about it, I went along with it. I dreamed about becoming a member of Chi Kappa Sorority.

Here was my logic: When Kim quit, I thought that maybe Chi Kappa would look my way. I'm a senior and that has prestige, and I also have talent in drawing and painting. Chi Kappa doesn't have any artists as members, and I thought I might be good for their image. Still, I wasn't any good for *my* image, so why should they want me? They didn't.

I officially gave up my dream the day Elissa Hanes

approached me. Elissa's the smartest girl in Palm Canyon
High, and she and Kim decided to start a democratic
sorority in opposition, you might say, to the snobbish Chi
Kappa. They called their sorority The Pack. I found out
later that Pack stands for People Against Chi Kappa. It's
supposed to be a secret. I didn't tell too many people.

The Pack was still just a hope that day when Elissa
walked up to me. I was reading the notice that she and
Kim had put on the bulletin board. The notice said: "See
democracy at work. Join The Pack, a sorority." Then it had
Elissa's and Kim's names and phone numbers. Kim and
Elissa were watching me read the notice, but Elissa's the
one who took action.

The timing here was very important. Kim had quit at
the sorority's Thanksgiving dance. Tracy was still a member, and her mother, who's best friends with my mother,
immediately told my mother that I was being considered
to take Kim's place. I went into aggravation spasms won-
dering if it were true. But by the time I read the notice
about The Pack's forming, which was just a few days after
Kim quit, I already knew I was just fantasizing about Chi
Kappa's wanting me.

It's vital to me to remember what my frame of mind was
because I allowed Elissa Hanes to con me totally that day.
Elissa's a nice girl, but she has this really strong personality and I was ripe for being dominated.

Elissa said, "That's my notice, and Kim's. We're forming The Pack."

"Oh, great!" I said.

There it was, my enthusiasm problem. See, I didn't
know whether it was great to form The Pack or not.

Elissa was breathing on me. "Fritzi," she said, "our club

is in its infancy, and that's the best time to climb aboard. Later on it will get crowded, less . . . pristine."

I didn't know what *pristine* meant. "Is more or less pristine better? Never mind," I said.

Kim was looking at us but she didn't say anything.

Elissa was closing in on me. "Fritzi," she went on, "Kim and I are in the process of selecting officers for The Pack. The positions will go fast. They'll go to what you might call the pioneers, the early movers and shakers."

This was sounding pretty good. "Yeah?" I said. "Are you saying that if I join now, I could become an officer?"

"Not *could*. Will!"

Kim looked plenty surprised when Elissa said that, but she still kept quiet.

I wasn't any pushover. I said, "Um, I don't know, Elissa. Your sorority idea sounds *great*. It knocks me out, really. But I heard that Chi Kappa Sorority is considering me for its new tenth member. To replace you, Kim, you know, because you . . . resigned."

I said even more. I resisted. I really resisted.

But Elissa knew what she was doing. She told me straight out that the only way I'd ever get to be a member of any sorority, and an officer in addition, was to join The Pack.

Right there, in front of the bulletin board, I became a member, and the treasurer, of The Pack. If you don't count the founders, Elissa and Kim, *I* was Member Number One.

2

I broke the news to my mother when I got home from school that day. Breaking the news is the right expression. That's what you do when the news is bad. And for my mother, my joining The Pack was bad news.

"*The Pack?* What's that?" she asked in her Unidentified Flying Saucer voice, as if The Pack were not of this earth and not anything you could lay your hands on.

"It's this new sorority, Mom, that's a democracy. Anybody can join. It's much better than Chi Kappa, which is Snob City."

My mother has a rich, tanned, blond look that might make you think of Snob City. Not that she's a snob. But she definitely looks the part.

She said, "You weren't talking that way before. You were hoping that Chi Kappa would ask you to take Kim

Adler's place. And with Tracy McVane's being a member of Chi Kappa, I think you had a chance. You rushed into this, Fritzi. It's only been a few days since Kim quit."

"It's wake-up time, Mom. Like, reality is not as fabulous as unreality, but it's real. See, just because you and Tracy's mother are best friends doesn't mean that Tracy and I are anything special to each other. Tracy's editor of the school newspaper, she's one of the smartest girls in school, and we don't have much in common. We like each other—at least I *think* she likes me—but that's about it. I wish it were more but it isn't. And anyway, Tracy doesn't rule Chi Kappa. If they really wanted me, they would have asked me to join at the beginning of the school year when they had two openings. They filled them with girls who hadn't even lived in Palm Canyon for very long, Kim and that awful Crystal Jameson. Me, they ignored. I mean, I was Invisible City."

"And now Kim's quit," my mother said. "You see, they didn't pick a girl who'd be loyal to Chi Kappa."

"But Kim had this, like, *agony* reason for quitting. The sorority insulted her friend Elissa in public. At the sorority's Thanksgiving dance, you know."

"Yes, but quitting isn't the answer." My mother said this as if she knew everything.

So she nearly fainted a few months later when Tracy McVane decided that quitting was the answer to *her* problems with Chi Kappa Sorority. Carrie Reis did her dirty, and Carrie was helped along by Allie Grendler and Selena Vonder, two of the more obnoxious members. Tracy enjoyed quitting.

So then my mother said, "Quitting seems to be getting fashionable. Maybe there's something to it, after all."

That's what I was trying to tell her. My mother's smarter than I am, but I'm more shrewd. And I'm beginning to think that with all the things that come along in life that you have to deal with, it's better to be shrewd—that is, if you have to pick one over the other.

Tracy joined The Pack. That made nine of us. We had been picking up members along the way. I like listing off the names because it makes me feel like the pioneer that Elissa was talking about when she conned me into joining. Elissa, Kim, me, Stephanie Ortiz, Deena Fox, Holly Wood, Marlene Garcia, Bridget Jawinski, and Tracy. We decided to get our own jackets. I was asked to design the logo that went on the back. The Pack had *noticed* that I have artistic talent. They noticed *me*. They were my friends. By then, I wouldn't have joined Chi Kappa if they got down on their hands and knees and licked my sandals. I don't own boots.

I was happy. But one of the rules in high school is that a girl can't really be happy without having a boyfriend. That's not written down anywhere. It just *is*. And I wanted somebody, a guy to like me, a guy I could like. Not because of a stupid rule. In actual fact, some girls are too busy for boys; some girls are too independent for boys. Trouble was, none of *those* girls was Fritzi Tass.

But the king-queen business came along, and I didn't have to worry about a boyfriend any more. I had to worry about two boyfriends.

Here's a rule about life: You can go from too little to too much in an instant.

Another rule, a romance one: For every guy who finds you resistible, there are probably two out there who find you irresistible. Never waste time on resistible.

3

I was pitching headlong toward romance, but I didn't know it yet. These were the preliminaries: the business about voting for spring king and queen. Tracy had come up with this controversial idea of picking the king and queen's names out of boxes instead of its being a popularity contest. Rona Dunne had already won queen two years in a row, and it was a sure thing that she'd win again if it kept on being a popularity contest.

Tracy wrote an editorial in favor of her lottery idea for picking royalty. I drew a cartoon to go along with it. We made a hit.

But then the members of Chi Kappa came up with their own editorial, saying that Tracy's idea was the pits. Wow, it was war! But Tracy won, sort of. The school decided to try her royalty-from-a-box at this year's spring prom and see what happened.

I put my name in the voting box for queen. That was the idea. Vote for yourself if you want. But personally I didn't think you could make somebody popular just by plucking his or her name out of a box. Anyway, I figured that Rona would win again because she was such a star. Her name would still get on so many slips of paper, she'd have the best chance.

But listen, I could live with that, anyway, because I wasn't going to the spring prom where the names would be picked. You could still win king or queen even if you didn't show up at the prom, but face it, I wasn't going to win and I wasn't going to go. Nobody invited me. Even though I got some acclaim for my editorial cartoon, it wasn't enough to push me into popularity. Last year I actually went to the prom. This guy Chuck, who was my boyfriend in a very temporary sort of way before he graduated, took me.

This year, forget it.

The date of the prom crept closer. This was classic high school heartbreak stuff, not getting asked to the prom. I wasn't into classic high school heartbreak, so why did I feel so awful? I didn't want to be one of those girls whose life was over, finished, *dissolved* if she couldn't go to the prom. But I'm a human being and I was getting passed by.

I was feeling depraved or deprived—I'm not sure what the difference is there—when the phone rang one night. It was after supper. My parents were back to work. They own Tass Realty, a real estate agency they started when we moved to Palm Canyon from New Jersey. It's been super-successful, but sometimes the hours are weird. My folks have to show houses at their clients' convenience.

My sister, Brenda, and I both got to the phone at the same time. She's ten. She has three girlfriends she's always talking to on the phone, so I let her answer.

"Tass Residence. Brenda Tass speaking."

Who taught her *that?*

She handed me the phone. "It's for you. A guy. A real one."

Every year my parents say that next year Brenda will stop being bratty.

I took the receiver.

"Hello."

"Hi! Fritzi? My name is Seth Berns, and I hope I'm lucky enough to get you before some other guy invites you to the spring prom."

In one sentence? In one sentence everything changed for me. I didn't know Seth Berns from a hole in the wall. All I knew was that I didn't feel depraved anymore.

Deprived?

Whatever.

4

"**W**ho are you?" I asked.

I already knew. He was someone who must have *noticed* me. Here it was happening again. First The Pack noticed me and my talent, and now this Seth Berns must have noticed me and my—*what?* Attractiveness, I guess. He was asking me to the prom. But why wasn't the name Seth Berns familiar to me? Being a senior, I knew who most of the kids were by now. He must be one of those brilliant quiet types who stay apart from the crowd. I was multiplying how many times he had ogled me as I walked up and down the halls. Four years times maybe three times a day average . . .

"Peter Zee gave me your name."

He didn't even know me! So much for my multiplica-
tion tables.

"Peter and I are good friends," he went on.

I started to catch on. I had never met Peter Zee, but I'd
had some contact with him, so to speak. Carrie Reis had
been going out with him, but Tracy liked him too. And I
had some information that would set Peter straight that
Tracy was an okay person and Carrie was not. So naturally
I mailed this information to Peter. He goes to Wilmot
High, the other high school in town, which didn't make it
convenient to deliver the information in person. After
Peter read what I sent him he dumped Carrie and became
Tracy's boyfriend.

I did a good piece of work there. But it terrified Tracy.
She never did trust me with information, and then she
knew for sure why. Still, she was grateful to me, and we
started to become friends, just as our mothers had always
hoped.

Now I knew just how grateful Tracy was. She must have
told Peter to get me a date for the spring prom. And here
he was. Seth.

I wanted to play hard to get. But I didn't want to outwit
myself. I'll just be an untalkative person until I hear
everything Seth's got to say.

He said, "Are you there, Fritzi?"

"I am here."

"Well, I'd really like to take you to the prom. We could
double-date with Peter and Tracy, if that's okay with you.
But first I guess you want me to describe myself."

"Not necessary. Like, you're either going to over-
describe yourself if you're conceited or underdescribe
yourself if you're modest, and I already know you're not

going to hit the middle because nobody does. But you deserve the same offer you gave me. I'll describe myself if you want."

"Peter already told me about you. He raved. He said you're a loyal friend of Tracy's and you're a cartoonist . . . an artistic person."

"Raved, huh? I've never met Peter."

"He said you two have had some correspondence."

"Yeah, you might say that. Okay, Seth, let's do the prom together."

"Great. I can't wait to meet you."

He was on an admiration spree. I loved it!

The spree was over. He said, "I'll pick you up at—wait, I'd better check with Peter. We'll be going in his car."

After I hung up I wondered if he were one of those people you meet over the phone who sound like fun, but then you see them in person and it's as if you never talked on the phone at all. They're just strange and stiff and uptight.

Brenda was still near the phone. She had listened to everything from my end.

"Who is this guy?"

"His name is Seth, and I'm going out with him. And if you don't stop saying those wise-guy things when I get a phone call —"

"I didn't swear, did I? Count your blessings."

Suddenly Brenda hugged me. "You're going to the spring prom, aren't you? I heard you say 'prom.' That is *so* heavy. Let me help you pick out a dress. Please! Please!"

"Nothing doing. You'll tell everybody that you helped me pick out a dress. You, you're only ten years old."

"I won't tell anybody. You and Mom are the gossips in

the family, remember? And what difference does it make if I'm only ten years old? I have fabulous taste."

She does have fabulous taste.

The next afternoon, after school, Brenda and I went to the mall where she immediately found a gorgeous blue gown that had a big sash and a very wide skirt.

"It's you," she said to me.

It *was!*

# 5

**B**renda insisted on helping me get dressed for the prom. She tried hard to be helpful. That's the way she is: she's horrible or she's wonderful. You never know which side will be on top.

"I hope you have the best time," she said.

She was putting on my shoes. On herself.

"These almost fit me," she said. She took them off and handed them to me.

"If you don't have a good time, don't feel bad," she added. "Just remember that proms are basically stupid."

"What? You were all excited when I got invited."

"Sure. But that doesn't change the premise of proms. Never mind, this isn't the time to go into it."

"No, go into it. I'm interested."

"Okay, the premise is: I'll just *die* if I don't get an invitation. *Die*, do you hear me!"

Brenda fluttered her eyelashes.

The doorbell rang.

"He's here!" she said. "Want me to entertain him while you finish getting ready?"

"I'm finished. Don't I look finished?"

Brenda looked me up and down.

"If Tracy's hair is purple, you're gonna look awfully upstaged beside her. Your hair's just its usual curly self. You could flip it up or something."

"It's fine."

"What if Seth's a jerk?"

"Peter and Tracy wouldn't fix me up with a jerk."

"Maybe he's a jerk and they don't know it."

Brenda's bratty side was coming up for air.

I rushed to the door. I knew my parents weren't going to answer it. They were busy in their home gym. They have, among other things, a rowing machine, a chinning bar, weights, a jump rope, a stationary bike, and, of course, an exercise mat. They put all their efforts into making the gym nice, and they let the rest of the house go. The paint's peeling, the rugs are like dog-kennel rejects, and you'd never believe that anyone who looks like my mother would live here. But she doesn't even notice because she's so hung up on her gym. I mean, it's fine for her, but Seth's at our door, and what do I do—invite him into our *gym?*

I opened the door.

There he was. In a tux. He was holding a corsage. He had good posture but not stiff. His features were strong. Brown eyes, sandy-colored hair. A dozen girls, minimum, were interested in him at Wilmot High. This was my first impression.

"Hi," he said.

"Hi, Seth."

I wished I had flipped up my hair.

He motioned toward the car. Peter and Tracy were waiting for us. There wasn't any problem about inviting Seth inside. I waved to Brenda, who was waiting for Seth to step inside so she could give him an eye sweep.

"At last we meet," he said as we walked down toward the car.

You'd think he'd been waiting a century or something.

"At last," I said. That was easy to say. I usually don't have trouble talking, but I didn't want to mess up this blind date. By the time we reached the car, which wasn't a very long time at all, I raised my dozen-interested-girls estimate to two dozen minimum.

Tracy and Peter were in the front seat. The car light went on when Seth opened the door, and there was Tracy with plain brown hair and a tame gold dress. Tracy's hair was usually purple or some pink-orange combo or green, and it went out in all directions in a style you see on the Statue of Liberty's head, which I hear is also getting green. Tracy's clothes were usually wild too. Tracy must have turned brown-and-gold for this guy. It had to be love!

Peter was wearing a tux and the after-shave scent of a dozen meadows. Before anybody could say anything much, Seth climbed into the car after me and handed me the corsage he had been carrying. He probably forgot to give it to me at the door.

It was a beautiful arrangement of white flowers, but last year Chuck had given me a corsage, and he stabbed me with a pin and I got blood on my dress, and Chuck made first-aid jokes all night. I pinned Seth's corsage to my sash before Seth got a chance to do any pinning.

It seemed as if it took no time to get to the school. The Palm Canyon High gym was already filled with dancers. The band was jumping around while it played. I saw some of my friends from The Pack. Elissa was with her boyfriend Eric Day, and Kim was with her boyfriend Brett Fox. I also saw Holly and Marlene, but I didn't recognize their dates.

With all the kids on the dance floor, you'd think some of them would stop and notice the new arrivals. I wouldn't mind being noticed by as large an audience as possible. Stadium-size. Ladies and gentlemen, observe. Fritzi Tass here. With Seth Berns of Wilmot High. Aren't you watching?

They weren't. There is something about the bigness of a crowd that makes you zero in on the smallness of you. Oh, for once in my life to make an appearance and Crowd Control would have to be called in!

The band started to play something slow. Seth asked me to dance.

"Ever been to a dance here?" I asked him as we moved around the floor.

"No."

"What do you think of our gym?"

"I've seen the gym before."

"Oh."

How did we fall into bland blind-date talk? We had done much better on the phone.

I saw Peter and Tracy starting to dance. Then suddenly I saw this big bunch of glitter walk in. Every single member of the Chi Kappa Sorority, sequined to the teeth,

blazed in with their dates. All nine girls including Melanie Deborah Kane. Melanie's the one who replaced Kim.
She's just a freshman, but I heard that Chi Kappa took her
in as a kind of social experiment. Lots of luck, Melanie.
They hadn't replaced Tracy with a tenth member yet. But
wait till Carrie Reis saw Tracy with Peter. Carrie had
invited Peter to the prom, but he turned her down. Carrie didn't even know about Peter and Tracy's dating. Rona
Dunne was with Mitchell Brenner, the most popular guy
in school. That figured. The most popular girl with the
most popular guy. And to prove it, they'd probably get
crowned tonight.

I've had this crush on Mitchell Brenner all through my
high-school career, but so has almost every other girl at
Palm Canyon High. Once he said hi to me or to the girl
standing right in back of me, and it was, like, pathetic
while the girl and I tried to figure out to whom he was
talking. In the time we spent, Mitchell Brenner could
have said another hi and made us both thrilled to be alive.

Oh boy, fireworks! Carrie and her date, Sanford Fuller,
started to dance, and then Carrie discovered Peter with
Tracy.

"Move closer!" I said to Seth. "I can't hear what's going
on. I'm missing an important conversation."

Seth laughed. "It's all over. Carrie is dragging her date
away from Peter and Tracy."

"You know Carrie?"

"I met her once when she was with Peter."

"Did you double-date?"

"Yes."

"With a friend of Carrie's?"

"No, with a friend of mine."

I felt jealous of this friend of his who knew him better than I did, who maybe was his girlfriend, who probably didn't let her mother do most of her homework. This girl was way ahead of me.

"She's just a pal," he said.

"You're explaining her to me?" My old enthusiasm was coming back. "That is just the greatest thing to do. It's all voluntary. I didn't ask, did I? I don't ask personal questions. I take what's given to me. Now what can I tell you about me that you don't already know?"

Why had he explained that she was just a pal? He wanted me to know that she didn't mean anything to him. This girl—it must have killed her to be just a pal to him. Those are the breaks.

Seth was thinking over my question when Peter and Tracy danced our way. Tracy said, "Food. Let's get some."

We were a foursome again, and we talked about the things that four people might talk about instead of the things that two people, boy and girl, might talk about. And we ate. The food was wonderful, and I hoped it would all get eaten up so it wouldn't show up in another form in the cafeteria on Monday.

After we ate, we danced some more, and then suddenly it was plucking time. Time to pluck the names of the spring king and queen from the boxes. There was a drum roll.

"C'mon, Seth, I want to be with Tracy when the names are picked. This could be a disaster for her if two of the school's lowlifes are picked. We have a few real scuzzy characters in our school. Even worse, if Rona Dunne gets to be queen, it'll be like laughing in Tracy's face."

We were at the back of the crowd. Tracy and Peter were

near the front. It seemed as if everybody wanted to get nearer the front.

Mr. Middle, the teacher who was going to do the plucking, was standing beside two very big boxes. The boxes were in front of the band. On the other side of him were two snazzy gold crowns on a velvet-covered raised thing.

There was a mike in front of Mr. Middle, and he was fooling around with it to get it right. Then he said, "It's time to pick our royalty! Spring king, spring queen. Who will be the lucky winners?"

I saw Tracy looking around the room. She saw me, and I waved to her. Seth and I kept trying to move forward, but it wasn't working. I noticed that all the Chi Kappa girls were standing together on one side of the room.

Mr. Middle put his hand into one of the boxes. He pulled out a slip of paper. I wasn't ready for this, but he was. He made the announcement for king.

"MITCHELL BRENNER!"

"Whew! At least it wasn't a lowlife," I said to Seth.

"Is this guy Mitchell Brenner popular?"

Seth was curious.

"You better believe it. This guy's the most popular guy in . . . oh, no!"

"What's the matter?"

"Don't you see? It's just as we thought. *Feared.* The crowns are going to the most popular. Tracy's plan is turning into mush."

"The guy's popular, all right. I can see that now. He's getting handshakes and slaps on the back . . ."

"And a kiss from Rona Dunne," I said. "In a minute she'll expect a kiss back from him when she gets to be queen."

Mitchell went up and stood beside Mr. Middle. Mr. Middle said to him, "And now for your queen."

Into the second box went Mr. Middle's hand. He was having fun. He pulled out a piece of paper. Here we go!

But Mr. Middle kept looking at the paper. Or it seemed that way to me. From where I was standing I couldn't see Rona's face, but I could see Carrie's hand on her shoulder. Victory awaits.

Mr. Middle made his announcement.

"FRITZI MELVINA TASS!"

Oh, no! I never even thought about *my* actually winning!

Seth looked at me. Amazed.

Everybody was silent. The shock was thorough and complete throughout the room.

I had to say something.

"*Me?*"

What should I do? I couldn't resign. It was too soon. I wasn't even crowned yet. Besides, queens don't resign. They abdicate. That much I knew.

Seth put his arm around me. "Congratulations, Queen Fritzi," he said.

He was proud of me just because I was lucky. I had to think about that.

And, it's to die, but there was Mitchell Brenner, *holding out his hand to me*. No question this time. There wasn't any girl behind me to discuss whether Mitchell was aiming for her or for me.

I walked forward.

6

**M**itchell and I were standing side by side. Mr. Middle placed a crown on Mitchell's head, and then a crown on mine. From nowhere a woman appeared with a ton of flowers and placed them in my arms. They crushed my corsage, but I couldn't do anything about it.

Then the cheers rang out. Stuff like: "Hooray for our royalty. Long live the king. Long live the queen. Speech, speech!"

Mitchell motioned to the crowd to be calm. I couldn't do it. I was holding all those flowers.

Then he said, "I'm happy to be your king and thank you."

He seemed to be a little embarrassed, and I thought that was good. Like, it's human.

It was my turn to say something. I was going to repeat his speech, only exchange king for queen.

But a girl in the crowd yelled, "Lucky Fritzi!"

The voice came from where the Chi Kappa girls were standing, but I couldn't tell who said it.

Nobody yelled that Mitchell was lucky.

I was mad.

Everybody was waiting for me to say something. I stepped close to the mike. I wanted to make sure I was heard.

I said, "I surely am lucky. I mean, if my name weren't picked by chance out of that box, I wouldn't be your spring queen. But actual fact is that my name *was* picked and I *am* your queen. Now, if you think that's some kind of *joke* because you wouldn't have picked me on your own, well, you can scrap that idea right now. And if you think I'm going to be your scapegoat person just because you didn't get the queen some of you wanted . . . well, forget it. Any school or any society that needs a scapegoat is in plenty of trouble. I think Palm Canyon High School can be better than that. Now, I consider being queen an actual job. I don't know how much power I have but—and no whistles or wisecracks—anything I can do for you to help the school, well, I'll try, and Mitchell will too."

I had my nerve including Mitchell, but he was king, wasn't he? He was absolutely stupefied by what I was saying. He kept looking at me. He scratched his head. He forgot he was wearing a crown. It tilted.

I finished up. "So now that I've set everything straight, thank you for any support you can give me."

Somebody in the crowd yelled, "Yea, Fritzi!" Then everyone seemed to be cheering. Tracy looked as if she were yelling her lungs out. This was a victory for her too.

It was so hard to believe that all of these kids were cheering for me. Could Crowd Control be far behind?

Mitchell put his hand on my shoulder. "You're something else," he said.

Again there was no girl behind me.

He admired me. I could see it in his face, I could feel it on my shoulder. I thought I was going to pass out. Suddenly it was all too much.

"Don't we get to sit down?" I asked him. "Shouldn't we have thrones or something?"

"I'll get you a chair," he said.

He took off but didn't get very far. Rona grabbed him. I could see that he was trying to explain something to her, but meanwhile, sort of out of nowhere, just like my garden of flowers, a chair was produced for me. Mitchell saw it, shrugged, and smiled at me.

The music resumed, and Rona led Mitchell to the dance floor. But it seemed as though most of the kids came rushing up to me instead of dancing: Tracy, Peter, Seth, members of The Pack, and loads of kids I hardly knew.

But not everybody was on a worship trip. The members of Chi Kappa were giving me cold looks. They hated me for being queen, for pushing out Rona. They could have hated Fate, but they picked me instead.

I should care. Mostly everybody else seemed to love me. It all got to be a blur. I sat in my chair, surrounded. Seth leaned down and kissed me on the forehead. That's the last personal thing I got from him all night, except a kiss at my front door in full view of Tracy and Peter.

Is there such a thing as being too popular?

It was just crazy what happened next. It began at school the next Monday. In the cafeteria. Here's the setup there: Chi Kappa has its own table, which is known as Buckingham Palace. I mean, it's very *very*. But now The Pack had started *its* own table, which doesn't have a name. If somebody who isn't a Pack member wants to sit at their table, it's okay because The Pack not only claims to be a democracy, it acts like one. But nobody ever tries to invade Buckingham Palace.

We have staggered lunch hours at Palm Canyon High, so usually not all the members of either sorority are in the cafeteria at the same time. On Monday at The Pack's table, when I was there at lunch, we also had Kim, Tracy, Elissa, and Deena. At Chi Kappa's table Rona, Carrie, and Daisy Baron—who is one half of the Baron twins— were eating.

"It's our queen," Elissa said when I arrived at The Pack's table. Then she and Kim and Tracy and Deena clapped. We had been through the congratulations stuff already. The Pack members who were at the prom congratulated me there, and the others phoned me the next day. So now they were clapping a little for themselves and as a slap at Chi Kappa. The cafeteria was a place where battles were fought.

Naturally I felt like queen of the school, which in fact I was. I cannot describe the thrill. Finally I was noticed, I had respect. Getting my name picked from the box got me noticed, but giving that speech got me respect. Here's a bold thought: If the kids were voting for queen now, in the old style, a popularity contest, I think I'd have a good chance of winning *that* way. One minute an underdog, the next minute an overdog.

Seth had already asked me for another date, which I accepted. He'd asked me at the door when he'd said good night on the night of the prom. I knew he would, I just knew it. But now, at school, I was looking around for Mitchell to see what would happen next with him. If anything. I didn't see him.

Anyway, lunch was great, but it's what happened after lunch that really threw me. I was walking toward the cafeteria exit when suddenly Rona Dunne was beside me. Listen, I knew the cafeteria was a battleground, but she wouldn't do anything bodily to me on the premises, would she?

"Fritzi," she said, "I just want to congratulate you on becoming queen. I know how it feels. I was queen for two years in a row."

What a turnaround! At the prom she was something like furious, it seemed to me. But we all know that Rona's cool. Now she was *very* cool. She had a hidden reason for what she was saying to me.

I answered, "Thanks." It was safe enough to say.

I started to walk faster.

"Wait," she said, catching up. "Don't you think we queens should stick together? We've got so much in common."

"We have?"

"Of course. This is a distinct honor. It's a very small club, you might say, just you and me. The girl who was queen before me graduated three years ago. That leaves just us."

This was confusing! I was thinking motives, intrigue. What did Rona really want?

"We've got a few minutes before the next class. Want to take a walk outside?" she asked.

"Well . . ."

"Come on."

"Well, all right."

Believe me, I was getting more and more curious.

We went outside. The weather was hot. Spring in Palm Canyon means blasts of hot air in the middle of the day.

"Fritzi," Rona said, "you know we wanted you as a member of Chi Kappa."

"No, I didn't know that."

What was she pulling here?

"Yes, it was after Kim Adler resigned. But you joined

The Pack so fast that we didn't have a chance to ask you."

I stopped walking. "Rona, take that garbage and drop it in the trash compactor."

Rona kept cool. She shook her blond head back and forth. "No, it's the truth. How do you know it isn't the truth?"

Actually I didn't.

But I said, "There are some things you just *know*, Rona."

"But, my dear Fritzi, that's so rash of you. You're taking a *notion* that you, or possibly Elissa, came up with, and you're saying it's *fact*. I'm saying that you never gave Chi Kappa a chance."

"Okay, let's say that you're telling it to me straight. Why did you want *me?* I'm talking pre-queen."

"Isn't it obvious, Fritzi? You're colorful, you're artistic, and I must confess that sometimes I think Chi Kappa is just a bit too laid back. We could use your *enthusiasm*."

I kept quiet. I was trying to think.

Rona had no problems that way. She knew exactly what she was doing. "You notice, Fritzi, that we took in Melanie Deborah Kane, a freshman. That's just one example of how we're trying new things. We're really looking hard at ourselves because we know we're not perfect. We're open to improvements, to new ways of doing things."

"Rona, like I'm still thinking 'trash compactor' with what you're saying. The other night at the prom, you Chi Kappa girls stayed away from me and gave me mean looks. You hated my getting queen."

We stopped walking and sat down on a wall.

"You're absolutely right, Fritzi. I admit I was disappointed when I didn't become queen again. There was my boyfriend, Mitch, the king, and it seemed only natural for me to be his queen."

*Her boyfriend, Mitch.* That sounded terrible to me. But it was true. Everyone knew that he and Rona dated regularly. Rona had him sewed up.

She smoothed her dress and wiggled her toes inside her sandals. Then she went on.

"So I was hurt, Fritzi. But what's important is that I snapped right back. Your being queen brought home to me how very much we had wanted you in Chi Kappa."

"Okay. So those are the breaks. I'm a member of The Pack."

"That's not forever, though."

"No, I'm going to graduate from high school in a few months."

"I meant that it's not forever while you're still going to Palm Canyon High. There's no law that says you have to stay in The Pack."

What was she getting at?

"You want me to kick The Pack in the teeth?" I asked.

She kept wiggling her toes. "Fritzi, we all talked this over at our meeting last night, and we want you to join Chi Kappa Sorority. To take Tracy McVane's place. We usually send a written invitation, but the circumstances are unusual here, so I'm asking you in person."

A person could fall off the wall with an invitation like that!

Suddenly Rona stepped down from the wall. "Don't answer me now," she said. "Just remember that we wanted you and we still do."

She walked away. She knew what to say and when to stop saying it.

But I couldn't believe what *I* was thinking! She had planted seeds in my mind about how Chi Kappa had been wanting me for a long time. But so what? Even if—big *if*—Chi Kappa had wanted me so much, the girls in The Pack were now my friends. They were my sorority sisters.

I walked to class slowly. I remembered how it once would have meant everything to me to have been asked into Chi Kappa Sorority.

I hoped it still didn't mean something.

**8**

**T**racy cornered me after my English class. "What did Rona want?"

"Nothing much."

"Fritzi, Fritzi, Fritzi, Rona never wants *nothing much!*"

"Okay, here it is. First she told me how much she and I have in common because we're both queens. Then she told me that Chi Kappa had wanted me as a member to replace Kim Adler but that I joined The Pack so fast, they didn't have a chance to invite me. She said they still want me. They want me to fill the vacancy you made when you quit."

Tracy laughed. "That lady is nuts. What a liar!"

"You mean she's lying that she wants me now, or lying that she wanted me before I joined The Pack?"

"The whole thing."

"But, Tracy, if she doesn't want me now, why would she actually invite me? What if I said yes? Then she'd be stuck with her invitation. Really stuck. Glue City."

Tracy shrugged. "Oh, I don't know why she did it. I think it's just a big joke or something. Forget it."

"I gave a speech at the prom about jokes. Doesn't Rona know better?"

Tracy shrugged again. "Who knows? Forget it. Gotta go to class. See you later."

Tracy, being smart and the editor of the school paper, should have been able to solve the Rona puzzle for me. But instead she got me kind of frustrated. Nobody plays a joke on Queen Fritzi, if it were a joke. Tracy just brushed this thing off, but I knew it deserved attention. I had to get more information.

And I knew how to go about it.

After school, outside, I saw Daisy Baron with her twin sister, Tulip. The flower twins. It wasn't any chance happening that I saw them. I had been waiting for Daisy. She was the softest member of Chi Kappa.

Daisy Baron was part of my scheme to gather information. I picked this daisy, but I had to be very careful that she didn't find out.

"Hey, Daisy," I called.

I shouldn't be doing this. I really shouldn't be doing this. Going after the weakest link in a chain is not the sporting thing to do.

But I hear it works.

**D**aisy and Tulip Baron looked at me in surprise. Then they both came over. No surprise there. They're known as a package deal. They're identical twins. Daisy got into Chi Kappa Sorority because the sorority basically wanted Tulip. You don't get Tulip without Daisy. Of all the members now left in Chi Kappa, I thought that Daisy was the best. That was Tracy's opinion too. Daisy mostly just seemed to go along with what the sorority did. She was her sister's ditto mark.

Even though the twins are identical, I could tell them apart because Daisy wore glasses. Also, Tulip fixed herself up more carefully. Daisy didn't seem to care about make-up and stuff. They both have straight dark hair that was gleaming under the sun as they stood in front of me.

I knew that Tulip would speak first. Tulip's bold and smart, and Daisy's shy and smart.

"What's up?" Tulip asked.

"Nothing much. I brought my car today, and I thought if you girls didn't bring yours, I'd give you a ride home."

They looked puzzled. I had never offered them a ride before. I had never really had anything to do with them before.

But then Tulip smiled as if she had caught onto something. "Ah, Rona spoke to you! And you said yes."

"About what?"

I wanted to be sure what she meant.

"About joining Chi Kappa. And now you're starting to make friends with the girls. Like us." Tulip smiled.

If this were a joke, it looked as if all the members of Chi Kappa might be in on it.

Daisy didn't say anything. Her green eyes, which are the same color as mine, were squinting under the sun. This must be a meeting of the green-eyed people.

My mind was drifting. I had to remember my goals.

Tulip looked at her watch. "I'd love to talk, but I'll be late for my meeting of the French Club."

This I knew. I knew Tulip belonged to the French Club and Daisy didn't. It was one of their few nonditto situations. I also knew that the French Club met at this time after school.

Tulip looked at Daisy. I wondered if that were something like looking in the mirror. "Daisy, if you go home with Fritzi, I'll take our car. Then I won't have to hitch a ride with one of the French-Club kids. Thanks, Fritzi, for the offer."

Tulip walked off without giving Daisy a chance to say what *she* wanted to do.

"Come on," I said to Daisy. "If I can find my way out of the parking lot, I'll take you straight to your door."

"This is nice of you, Fritzi."

Daisy walked along with me, her head slightly bent, shielding her from the sun or some unseen fear, maybe.

I said, "Glad to do it. I'm just so excited about everything, about getting to be queen, and now about Chi Kappa's wanting me for a member."

"You're excited about Chi Kappa's wanting you for a member?"

"Yeah, they do want me, don't they?"

I turned toward her, watching her expression carefully. Like, I'm a whiz at this stuff—this is where I shine. But I wasn't too crazy about unleashing my genius on Daisy Baron. She seemed like Miss Innocent.

She answered, "Yes."

"How do you know?"

"I'm a member."

"And you discussed it at the meeting last night, about asking me in?"

"Yes."

Oh, save me from dead-on-delivery answers! I needed details.

"Must have been some discussion," I said.

"Why?"

And above all, save me from rising-from-the-dead questions. I was in charge here, wasn't I? *I* asked the questions. And here was my trick one: "Like out of the blue the sorority wants me?"

I had to find out why the sorority wanted me and when it all started.

"Well, Chi Kappa does want you," Daisy said.

She said it as if the sorority were something apart, as if she weren't a member.

I wasn't getting anywhere.

"You're going to join?" she asked. "You're actually going to quit The Pack and join Chi Kappa?"

If I weren't careful, I'd be telling *her* things. I, who was so talented in the getting-information field.

"Who knows," I said.

"It's something you'll have to think about very carefully. Isn't it?"

"Yeah. But I haven't even thought about thinking about it. In other words, I have nothing to say."

"It must be a thrill being spring queen," Daisy said.

The subject was like very cleanly changed, and that was that. She got nothing from me, and I got nothing from her, except the feeling that maybe this weren't a joke. *If* she had filled me in with the details, then I would have known for sure.

I drove her up to her house. It was a multilevel house. I could see that from the outside. We don't have too many of those in Palm Canyon. Mostly everything's on one floor.

She didn't invite me in. The Baron house was kind of private, from what I'd heard. Her parents didn't mix much socially. No matter how busy my folks were with their business, they still were big at the golf course and other places where people got together. It was good for their business, I think. I didn't know what the Barons did, but whatever it was, they kept it pretty much quiet. It must be great to live in a place like Palm Canyon and stick up your nose at the golf courses and tennis courts and country club. But they raised Tulip, who needed Chi Kappa, and they raised Daisy, who needed Tulip, so they didn't completely have their act together.

Daisy thanked me for the ride and said, "Think slowly."
What did she mean by that?

When I got home, there wasn't any time to think about my next move. Brenda was waving the telephone receiver and saying, "It's your king. He's summoning you."

10

I raised my hands, as if I were going to strangle Brenda. She should be banned from answering phones!

But I was too happy to kill her. Mitchell Brenner was calling me!

I grabbed the receiver from Brenda.

"Hi," I said.

"Hi, Fritzi. How are you enjoying your royal station in life?"

"I'm enjoying. How about you?"

"It's fun. Aside from the kidding."

"You're getting kidded? I take this seriously. It's no joke."

"I know. That speech you gave was fantastic."

"Thanks."

Why was he calling? Just to check in with his queen, or did he have something else in mind? I wanted this con-

40

versation to last. What if it were just a polite how are you, good wishes on being queen, nice talking to you, and good-bye?

"Fritzi . . ."

He was hesitating.

"Yes?" I said in what I hoped was an urging-on voice.

"Fritzi, I was thinking that it would be a good idea for you and me to get together and talk about our being king and queen and try to come up with some new ways to help the school. Just as you said in your speech. In past years the king and queen were just figureheads. Maybe we can change that, you and I."

"You and I?" I repeated.

"Sure. If you've got some time now, I could drive by, pick you up. Maybe go over to Gregory's Galley for a sandwich?"

Was this a business call? Hard to figure. If it were, it could be the first time in history that a king telephoned a queen to arrange a royalty business talk in a place called Gregory's Galley. Why, I asked myself, did he pick that restaurant when there are so many teen hangouts around town? Gregory's Galley is mostly a place where adults eat, although Tracy and Peter went there once for dinner and the comedy show that's held there.

"I thought Gregory's Galley was just a restaurant for an older crowd to have dinner."

Why was I making a big deal out of the restaurant?

"Well, they'll take anybody's money," he said. "And it's open for lunch too. And all afternoon."

"Okay."

"You're free right now?"

"Yeah."

"Pick you up in fifteen minutes?"

"Yeah."

"Great. See you then."

I hung up.

"Yippee!!"

Brenda had been standing there listening, of course. I was so excited, I broke one of my privacy rules and talked to her. "My high-school career was meant to be boring up to these last few months," I said, "so that when these last few months came, I could appreciate them the way a starving person appreciates a good meal."

"A good meal at Gregory's Galley?"

"Yes, you nosy little twerp, yes!"

"That's for old people. Why is he taking you to a place for old people?"

"I don't know. That doesn't mean anything."

"Maybe it means something."

"What could it mean? Peter took Tracy there once. Sometimes kids go there, I guess."

"For the comedy show. But not in the afternoon."

"How do you know? You've got a guard hired outside to see who goes in? Maybe he thinks it's a good place to take a queen."

As I said this my excitement went dead. This could be just a formal kind of thing, like maybe Mitchell thought it was *expected* of him to do something like this, getting together with the girl who's queen. He'd do it and then he'd be finished.

I didn't change my clothes or anything like that. If Mitchell noticed me at school today, he'd know what I had been wearing, and then he'd know I changed my clothes just for him. My mind is smart when it comes to things like that. If I could pick the subjects I take at school, pick all of them, I could walk off with some of the best marks in the senior class. Art; investigative work; speech, maybe, if the content were more important than the language; and a few other talents I was now trying to develop. Like human relations, such as not killing my bratty sister.

Brenda was still standing there.

"If you have any bright ideas about answering the door when he comes," I said, "forget it. Now you just go and do whatever you'd be doing if you were minding your own business instead of mine."

Brenda started to move away. She stopped. "He's cute, isn't he? I heard he was cute, this Mitch."

"His name is Mitchell."

"Call him Mitch. It's more cozy."

"Leave!" I said.

When I opened the door for him fifteen minutes later, I said, "Hi, Mitch."

You don't throw away a good suggestion just because it comes from Brat City.

11

**G**regory's Galley was almost deserted. There were a few waiters hustling around setting things up, straightening things out. It was as if Mitch and I had arrived a few hours too soon for a party. I knew that the place got packed at night for dinner and their comedy show, but right now it seemed kind of odd to be there. Tracy had told me that the waiters wore funky clothes. But these waiters were dressed in shirts and jeans, which also made it seem as if we arrived before the waiters had a chance to put on the right clothes.

One of them led us to a booth. There were empty tables and empty booths. Our booth was in a corner. The waiter handed us menus.

"I feel like ice cream," I said. I was wiggling my feet in my sandals just as Rona had done. Summer had already arrived for my feet. That's where I feel the heat first. Why

44

couldn't Palm Canyon have a spring that felt like spring? Spring in New Jersey, which was fading in my mind, had been soft and warm in a cool sort of way.

"A sundae or a soda?" Mitch asked.

"Just plain ice cream in a dish. Vanilla, please."

"I'll have the same," Mitch said.

"Two vanillas," the waiter said, and he scooted off. I think he was wearing track shoes.

Here I was. With him. Sitting in a booth. Brenda had said he was cute. I guess when you're ten, everybody's cute. Or gross. Mitch has thick dark hair and deep brown eyes and broad shoulders and a deep voice like an actor's. Rona was probably crazy about him. Rona! This was the first time I had thought about her since he called. Was it okay for me to be out with him? I guess it depended on whether this were an actual date or a royalty consultation.

"Is this a royalty meeting?" I asked. I just had to know.

He tapped on the table with his fingers. "Well, it would be innovative if you and I, as queen and king, could come up with some ideas that would really make an impact on the school."

"So this *is* a royalty meeting?"

The waiter brought our ice creams. Fast. He was definitely wearing track shoes.

The ice cream wasn't going to taste all that great. I was beginning to get the reason behind this meeting, and the disappointment could wreck a person's appetite. Mitch was probably embarrassed out of his socks to be king, and so he was latching on to what I had said about making something good out of it. What did I expect, anyway? He was Rona's boyfriend, and I was just the girl who got lucky and got crowned beside him.

He ate three spoonfuls of ice cream before he answered me. "No, this isn't just a royalty meeting," he said. "Sure I'd love it if we could come up with some plan to put our so-called royal positions to good use. But the real reason I called you is because I'm very much attracted to you."

He put down his spoon and really, really looked at me.

I really, really thought I was going to die. No, not die. Live! Dying is what I was doing previously. He wasn't waiting for me to answer. He had more to say.

"Fritzi, I hardly knew you existed until you became queen. Then, while you were making that speech, something happened. I felt such admiration, such an attraction to you. But Rona took over at that point, if you recall, and I never had a chance to say anything to you."

This was too much for me! I said the first thing that came into my head. "How come you didn't look for me at school today and tell me?"

"I couldn't. Well, obviously I could have said something, but we couldn't have talked at any length."

"Why?"

"Don't you know?"

I knew. "Rona?" I said.

"That's it. That's why I invited you here where we wouldn't be seen by anyone we know. Rona and I go steady. I haven't taken out any other girl, or even looked at another girl, since Rona and I began dating. But now . . ."

Oh, the excruciating agony and wonder of it all. *I* was the other woman!

But I had my standards.

"I don't want to steal any other girl's boyfriend. See, I wouldn't want anyone to steal my boyfriend."

"You have a boyfriend? The guy with you at the prom?"

"He was a blind date. We're going out again this Saturday night, but this will be our first date with his knowing me."

Mitch dug into his ice cream again.

He said, "He must have liked you or he wouldn't have asked you out."

"Well, you know, it's hard to figure. Would it have been the same if I didn't get to be queen? We were getting along fine before that, but afterward he was really impressed." I took a spoonful of ice cream. "I shouldn't be telling you this. I mean, whatever Seth—that's his name—thinks of me, I shouldn't be talking about it with another guy."

"I'm talking about Rona with you."

"I know. And, like, it bothers me. Not a whole lot, though. Just being honest with you, Rona is not one of my favorite persons. Now she's suddenly friendly with me and I can't figure out why. She gave me reasons, but I'm going to find my own."

Should I tell him I was asked into Chi Kappa Sorority? No, wait on that. Anyway, why was I thinking about Rona? Mitch wasn't her prisoner, and he liked me so much, he was willing to . . . willing to . . . do what?

"Like, this is Confusion City," I said. "Rona is your girl friend but you're meeting me on the sly?"

"Yes. I'm not going to try to word that differently. It's true, just the way you said it."

The way Mitch was looking at me made it seem as if it were okay. But how did he feel about Rona? Can you suddenly stop liking or loving a girl you've been dating steadily?

I was curious enough—*Fritzi* enough—to ask.

"Okay, you're attracted to me, but how do you feel about Rona?"

"I have a lot of feeling for her. I can't just turn off those feelings, and maybe I never will. I just don't know."

I was gulping my ice cream. I was, like, agitated.

I asked, "Is this in the category of having your cake and eating it too? My mother's big on that expression, but it sure seems to fit this situation."

"I don't want it to be in that category, as you put it. This isn't something I went out and looked for. This is just something that happened. Almost in a flash. You can be pretty irresistible."

There it was. A guy who was either slinging me a tired, old line or a guy who really found me irresistible.

I went with the latter.

"Are you saying you want to see me some more?"

"Of course."

"You know I'm going out with Seth Saturday night."

"I'm going out with Rona."

"She gets you Saturday nights and I get you afternoons in a place where nobody sees us? That's the pits."

"It's temporary. You'll see how you feel and I'll see how I feel."

"Rona would hate me if she knew. First I took queen away from her, and now I'm taking her boyfriend."

"Fritzi . . ."

Mitch put his hand on mine.

"You didn't take anything from Rona, Fritzi. The queen thing was just chance, you know that. And you didn't make one move in my direction. If I stop being Rona's boyfriend, it won't be because *you* instigated it."

"But I'm not stopping it. I'm not backing away."

Mitch squeezed my hand. "Does that mean you'll see me again?"

"Uh-huh."

I let my hand stay under Mitch's until he took it away. Then I finished my ice cream. I needed something cool. I was in this hotbed of intrigue. Mitch, Seth, Chi Kappa, The Pack. I didn't know just where I fit in any more. It wasn't a case of not fitting in, it was a case of fitting into *too* many places.

It was the most wonderful problem I had ever had.

**E**verybody was home for supper. Sometimes Brenda eats at a girl friend's house and sometimes my folks eat at odd hours when they work odd hours.

My mother and father were of course thrilled that I got to be spring queen, and Brenda added to their thrill by reporting that King Mitch Brenner had taken me out that afternoon.

"Fritzi," my mother said over her roast beef, "you are coming into your own. You may have gotten off to a slow start in high school —"

"Three years plus several months of no action is a slow start?" Brenda asked. "If that's slow, what do you call stationary?"

"Brenda," my father said, "just because your marks are good and your mouth is incapable of slowing down does not mean that your comments are appreciated."

Dad lets Brenda have it like that a lot, but it doesn't do any good. Brenda's brilliant in school and it's gone to her head.

Which reminded me of something.

"Mom, I've got more good news."

"You're just overflowing with it, aren't you?" Mom smiled at me while she attacked her baked noodles.

"This good news is especially for you. I'm going to lighten your work load. You won't have to do my homework any more. Queen Fritzi does her own."

Mom put down her fork. "Now don't be drastic, Fritzi. I've been encouraging you to do your own work, but —"

"I'm not drastic. And I think the word is *impetuous*. I've been starting to look things up. I have to see how I'll do on my own again. I'm not going to college, anyway, and —"

My father interrupted. "Don't say that, Fritzi. One never knows."

"This one does. I want to get a job drawing or painting. Maybe doing ads in a department store or something. I'll have to start looking this summer."

"Not a bad idea. Take a year off and get your feet wet. Work. Then go to college the next year."

He didn't understand. Or maybe he did but didn't want to. "Dad, I'm not thinking college *ever*. Get it? Brenda will go to college for you. For the family honor."

I was sorry I said that. I didn't want to hurt my parents. But my future was *my* future.

Brenda actually tried to help. "If I had a talent for art the way Fritzi does, I might not go to college, either.

Fritzi's serious about her art. She's not just going to toss buckets of paint at a canvas and stand back and see what happens. But, Fritzi, if you do decide to do that, that's where the money is. All these intellectual types study the splashed paint and decide what it means and how much they'll pay for it."

Mom frowned. "I think we've exhausted this subject," she said. "And besides, I want to hear about Mitch Brenner. He took you out, Fritzi?"

"Not exactly out. Well, yes, in a way. But it's supposed to be a secret. Please don't say anything to your lady friends about it."

"Why not?"

"I can't tell you."

"But —"

I knew how to stop the questioning about Mitch Brenner. Just give Mom some information that would blow her mind.

Here it comes.

I took a bite of roast beef, chewed it slowly, and said, "I was invited to join Chi Kappa Sorority today."

That was definitely mind-blowing. Mom was electrified. Dad was electrified. Brenda was electrified.

"I don't understand," Mom said. "But I guess it must have something to do with your becoming queen?"

"I don't know. It's a puzzle. Rona Dunne approached me. She wants me to fill the spot left by Tracy's quitting. She even told me that Chi Kappa had wanted me when Kim Adler quit but that I joined The Pack before Chi Kappa had a chance to ask me."

"Incredible!" Mom said.

"This is your dream come true, Mom. An invitation

from Chi Kappa. Remember how much you wanted it for me?"

"I remember."

"So? How does this strike you?"

"Like a dagger through the heart. No, through the back. There's something wrong about this, about the timing. You don't need those Chi Kappa girls any more, Fritzi. You don't want them. The Pack is your sorority."

My father joined in. "I agree with your mother, Fritzi. So what are you going to do?"

"I'm gonna find out what's behind Chi Kappa's invitation."

"That's easy," said Brenda. "They simply want the queen. Sometimes ulterior motives don't have any ulteriors."

My mother looked concerned. "You *are* sticking with The Pack, aren't you?"

"Sure."

"It must be so exciting for you simply walking into that school now, Fritzi. I only wish it had happened sooner. In your first year, for example."

"Now, Epsy," my father said, "just be happy with what she has."

I was happy with what I had. I looked forward to going to school now. I looked forward to doing my own homework again. I also looked forward to exchanging meaningful glances with Mitch. I loved secrets — other people's so I could find out what they were, and mine so I could keep them to myself.

Mitch and I did exchange some meaningful glances the next couple of days. I got big waves from the members of Chi Kappa, but nobody approached me. It was as if they

wanted to give me space to make up my mind about joining. And then there was The Pack. Tracy must not have
said one word to them about Chi Kappa's invitation to me,
because when I sat at The Pack's table for lunch, no one
brought it up. I guess Tracy really did think it was all a
joke to be ignored.

When I got home from school on Wednesday, Brenda
handed me an envelope with my name and address typed
on it. At least she didn't open my mail.

"This was in the mail for you," she said. "Want me to
screen your fan letters from now on? You might be need-
ing a social secretary."

"If you ever read my letters —"

I took the envelope to my room and looked at it. There
was no return address on it.

I opened the envelope. There was a small piece of
paper folded inside. I took it out. There was a message
typed on it: "DON'T DO IT. YOU'LL BE SORRY."

I sat down on my bed. This was threatening stuff!

In my whole life I had never received a threatening
note or a threatening phone call, even as a joke. And this
note was no joke. It was straight to the point and it meant
business.

But what did it *mean?* What shouldn't I do? About what
would I be sorry?

What kind of complicated life was I living that I
couldn't even figure out to what a threatening note was
referring?

Maybe it was about joining Chi Kappa. What if Tracy
really didn't think their invitation was a joke? What if she
had told the other members of The Pack and they all got
together and wrote this note to me? Maybe that's why

they never said one word about the invitation at lunch.

Oh, boy, Fritzi Tass, like, living in New Jersey may have been a safer situation for you. Like being unpopular in Palm Canyon High may have been a safer situation. People who have too much—too much money, too much popularity, too much something or other—probably get a higher percentage of threatening notes than the regular population.

Could the note be from Rona? What if she found out about Mitch and me? This could be Rona's way of trying to scare me off. Rona's not the type to come up to a person and beg for a guy.

But what if the note didn't have anything to do with the sororities or Mitch? *What if it were about something else?*

Maybe somebody out there didn't want me to be queen any more. Or in the first place.

What if somebody just plain hated Fritzi Tass?

The note could be about *anything!* The dummy who sent it should have realized that I have many interesting things going on in my life, and that a little accuracy, a few details, would be appreciated.

I allowed myself to be mad about that.

For a few minutes it kept me from being scared.

**13**

The note changed everything. I thought about it all the time. When I saw Mitch at school, I thought about it. When I saw the members of Chi Kappa, I thought about it. When I saw the members of The Pack, I thought about it. And worst of all, when I walked down the halls of Palm Canyon High and when I went to my classes, I thought about it. *Anybody* could have mailed that note to me. Even a stranger, some misfit at school who was out to get me.

I hadn't told anybody about the note yet. But I couldn't keep it to myself forever. It had been two days now, and I hadn't been able to come to any conclusions about it. I thought about going to the police. They would ask a million questions. They would draw my parents into it.

Maybe it was a joke, after all. Some juvenile's idea of

fun. A juvenile who would grow up to write negative for-
tune-cookie messages for a living.

The weekend was coming up. Cheers. I had a date with
Seth for Saturday night, and I wondered how it would be,
going out with him without Tracy and Peter along.

I was walking to my car in the school parking lot Friday
afternoon when Rona caught up with me.

"You've had a few days to think over my invitation," she
said. "What do you say?"

"As I told you before, I'm a member of The Pack."

She smiled. "We all *realize* that, Fritzi, and we've been
talking among ourselves and have come up with an idea
that's unprecedented. It's something we've never, never
done before."

Something they'd never done before? I had it. They
were planning to be civil to the girls who weren't members.

Rona put her hand on my arm. "Now, without any obli-
gation on your part, we'd like you to attend a meeting of
Chi Kappa Sorority. We've never allowed a nonmember
to attend before, but we're so sure you'll want to join after
you've shared this experience that we're making this phenomenal offer."

Rona had been reading too many ads: without any obli-
gation on your part; we're so sure you'll want to; we're
making this phenomenal offer. These were standard sales
pitches. You could sell a used car that way!

But I was tempted. She wanted me so much that I
wanted more than ever to find out why. Also, maybe I
could learn something about the note. That was a real
long shot, but who knows?

I hated myself, but I said, "Maybe."

"Marvelous. The next meeting?"

"When is it?"

"This Sunday night."

"The Pack's meeting this Sunday night. We don't meet every Sunday night, but this Sunday we've got a meeting scheduled."

"Perhaps you could get out of it?"

She smiled slickly.

Or was it sickly?

Why didn't I just say no!

Still, I wasn't this wonderful perfect person myself. I had agreed to date her boyfriend on the sly. It didn't seem that she knew about Mitch and me. If she didn't, I could drop her from my list of notewriting suspects.

At last I said, "I'll phone you on Sunday and let you know. Okay?"

"That's fine. And, of course, we're all hoping very much that you'll come. The meeting is at Melanie Deborah Kane's house."

"She's your newest member. She's having a meeting at her house already?"

"She's not that new. But, nevertheless, having meetings is one of the obligations of sorority membership. It's that way with The Pack, too, isn't it?"

"Yeah."

I sure knew about that one. I kept putting off having a meeting at my house. Elissa had already had a couple and so had Kim. Most of the other members each had one meeting. I kept making excuses for not having one at my house. My house was such a wreck. It needed new paint, new drapes, new carpeting, new appliances. Some house for real-estate people to be living in! But our gym was

gleaming, new, and fabulous. Perhaps I could hold a
meeting in the gym. One member could sit on the rowing
machine, one on the bicycle, a few could lie on the mat—
it could work. I knew that Tracy's house had a doorbell
that embarrassed her. It played "America the Beautiful."
But I had a whole house, with the exception of the gym.
Don't parents think about these things! My folks had
promised to fix our house "very soon," but they were
always too busy.

"So," Rona said, "you're thinking about my offer now?
Shall I tell the girls yes?"

"I said Sunday. I'll call you Sunday."

"Good enough," Rona said. "I'll hope for an affirmative
call."

She went to her car.

I went to mine. I got in and drove home.

When I got there, there was another envelope waiting
for me. I found it in the mailbox. Nobody was home.

I took the envelope into the house before I opened it.
But I had recognized the general look of the envelope. It
was like the last one.

I opened the envelope. At least it didn't contain a poi-
sonous snake or a dead creature labeled with my name.

It contained another note.

14

"**Y**OU REALLY WILL BE SORRY!**"

I was shaking as I read it.

It was time to tell somebody about the notes. This could even affect my family.

The telephone rang.

A threatening phone call to follow up on the note?

I said a weak hello.

"You sound terrible. Or is it the connection?"

"Mitch?"

"Mitch to the rescue. If something's wrong."

"Something's wrong."

"You can tell me all about it. I was calling to ask if you'd like to go for a drive."

"I'd love it."

"When's a good time for you?"

"Immediately. Immediately, please."

"Are you okay?"

"No."

"I'll be right over."

He hung up without saying good-bye.

I opened a bureau drawer and took out the first note, which I had hidden under some shorts.

I was glad that nobody was home. All I needed to have was Brenda to stick her nose into my business.

I decided to change into a pair of shorts and a halter. I felt hot.

I stuffed the two notes into the pocket of my shorts. Then I went outside to wait for Mitch. The outside of my house was attractive brick. But I didn't want Mitch to get a look *inside*. If I kept on seeing him, I couldn't avoid it. But one problem at a time.

I got into Mitch's car as soon as he drove up. He didn't kiss me hello. In fact, he hadn't kissed me yet. Maybe it had something to do with our situation's being a daylight one.

"Hi," he said. And he turned off the motor.

What was he doing?

"I think you want to talk," he said. "I think you want to talk right now. Driving and heavy conversation can be hazardous to your health, so let's just sit here and concentrate on your problem."

I should invite him into the house. It's not polite to sit outside here as if we're homeless when there's a house right here and I've got a key. But maybe he didn't care. Boys don't always think about etiquette-type things.

I took the two notes out of my pocket and handed them to Mitch. If he hadn't phoned when he did, I don't know to whom I would have shown them. Maybe my mother or father. Maybe Tracy. But what if the notes came from The Pack? What if they weren't meant to be menacing, only informative?

Mitch was reading the notes. "I got one today and one a couple of days ago," I said. "The one that says *really*, I got today."

His handsome face turned seriously handsome.

"Have you any idea who might have sent these?"

"No idea. Well, naturally I've thought about it, thought about, well, suspects—"

"And . . ."

"I thought maybe the notes had something to do with you and me and Rona."

"You mean that Rona sent them as a warning for you to stay away from me?"

"Could be. Or it could be a sorority thing. Rona invited me into Chi Kappa. She wants me to quit The Pack. I told Tracy about it. So maybe The Pack is trying to warn me."

"You think they'd write these notes?"

"You're talking eight girls, and it would take a lot of mind exploring on my part to see what's inside their heads. But I know Tracy has a strong personality and so does Elissa. They'd just come out and say what's on their minds. And anyway, Tracy said that Rona's inviting me is just some kind of joke."

"Well, I can tell you that writing notes isn't Rona's style, either. And besides, I'm sure she doesn't know anything about us." Mitch turned toward me.

"Fritzi," he said, and suddenly he leaned over and

brushed his hand through my hair. "I've made a decision about that, anyway. I'm not married to Rona, I'm not engaged to Rona. I want to tell Rona about you. I'd like to take you out openly."

"You're dropping Rona?"

"Honestly, no. I'd still like to take her out. But I don't want to deceive her, and I don't want to put you in that position, either. I respect you too much."

Respect! My favorite quality. I kissed him.

Our first kiss. And it came from me.

But I couldn't help myself, I was so happy.

I said, "This is just the best thing you could have said to me. Like, I've never been the other woman before and it can go to your head. But a few days being it, a week tops, is enough."

He put his arms around me. *He* was going to kiss *me* this time, and I knew it was going to be a good one. But I never found out because Brenda came walking up and, of course, looked straight in the car.

"Oh, hi," she said. "Excuse me, but I always check out strange cars. Fritzi, why don't you invite your friend in?"

"How would you like a ten-year-old sister?" I asked Mitch as Brenda walked away. "She's on sale this week for a nickel, but I'll drop the price if you're interested."

He laughed.

Actually I was killing time while I tried to figure out what to do. Mitch had called me up to take a drive, but it hadn't worked out that way. We also hadn't finished talking about the notes.

"Would you like to come in for something to eat?" I asked. The correct answer to that question was no.

"Oh, sure, if it's okay."

Maybe a house looks better to a stranger than to someone who's freaked out on its ugliness.

But no use taking chances.

"Would you like to see our gym?" I asked. "It's such fun to eat while you're sitting on the rowing machine."

**15**

**H**ere are Mitch's thoughts from the rowing machine about my notes: "Instead of thinking about them from a personal or emotional point of view, consider them scientifically. Look at them for clues."

Being an investigative-type person, I had already done that. But after Mitch went home I did it again. In mystery stories there's sometimes an odd-looking letter or figure or something that you can match up with a suspect's typewriter. But the typing on the notes and envelopes was ordinary and even. Sometimes there's something about the paper on which a note is written. But that didn't apply to my notes, either. Talk about boring paper, this was stuff you could buy anywhere. Plain, white, unlined, unmarked.

On to fingerprints. Fingerprints aren't what they're cracked up to be on TV shows. In real life fingerprints don't help to solve nearly as many crimes as they do on television. Besides, I didn't know if writing this note was a crime. Maybe it was a prank. Or even a pathetic attempt to say something that the writer was afraid to say in plain sight.

I put the notes back in my drawer. Maybe there wouldn't be any more. Besides, I had other things to think about. Like Mitch. He really liked me. But tomorrow night I'd be going out with Seth. I guess he really liked me too. A romantic battle could be raging over this situation. Two terrific guys fighting over me. I could bring out the Godzilla and King Kong in these fellows. And both sororities wanted me too. I had so much popularity, I wanted to give some of it away to the needy.

I thought of somebody who might be needy after tomorrow night. Rona. Tomorrow night Mitch was going to tell her about me. That could wipe them out. And it could wipe out Rona's inviting me into Chi Kappa Sorority.

Suddenly it seemed like a smart idea to call Rona about the sorority meeting *before* Mitch broke his news to her. I could avoid having Rona hang up on me and perhaps call me names I couldn't look up in the dictionary because they were nasty.

I looked up Rona's number in the phone book. I dialed it. She answered.

I said, "Rona, it's Fritzi Tass."

"You've decided?"

"Yes, I'm not going to the meeting."

"Which one? Chi Kappa's or The Pack's?"

"Chi Kappa's."

"Very well. But time's running out, you know. We'll have to pick our tenth member soon. Tell you what, I'll keep the invitation open for you for next week. The meeting that Sunday will be at the Baron twins' house. Try to come. But that's it. We'll be selecting another member that night if you don't show up."

"Did you say the Baron house?"

"Yes. Why?"

"I hear they're very private. Not much company."

"That's true. But every member has to have meetings, remember?"

"All too well."

Rona was beginning to give up on me, I could tell. But she didn't seem ready to hang up. She said, "Oh, by the way, Fritzi, I hear that you'll be looking for a job in a department store when you graduate. Doing ads."

I didn't ask her how she knew that. Most everyone knew by now.

She said, "My family has connections in Freeze's."

"Freeze's? Wow!"

"Yes, it's a fabulous store, and they do a tremendous amount of advertising, and most important of all, they like to train young people. But, of course, it's very competitive getting in, you know. Well, I've got a bunch of things to do, so I'll have to sign off. Have a nice weekend."

Rona was the coolest thing going. She dangled big bait in front of me and then pulled back. It was up to me to run after it.

I did *not* want to run after Rona's bait. I did not want to walk after it. I did not want to pay any attention to it. Please, temptation, pass me by!

What did it matter? Tomorrow night, after Mitch told her about me, she'd despise me. With any luck.

One problem solved.

16

I forgot what Seth looked like! How can that happen in just a week, forgetting what somebody looks like? But as I was getting ready for my date with Seth, I kept seeing Mitch's face in my head. I also forgot Seth's personality. Going blank like that in a week was scary. Maybe it happened to Seth too. Fritzi Tass could have become the forgotten woman.

I was staring at my crown. I kept it on my bureau, and every time I looked at it, I wondered where Mitch kept his. I didn't want to ask him in case he threw it out or something, and that would have crushed me because I valued mine so much. But now I was looking at my crown, hoping that it would bring back a vision of Seth Berns, the forgotten man. He was there when I was crowned, so I was trying memory by association.

I was ready for him, ready to sweep out the door when

he came. On Saturday nights you don't invite someone into your gym to wait for you. Besides, my parents were working out there.

When I saw Seth at the door, everything came back. I remembered him very well. He was dressed up, wearing a suit. The guys I know hardly ever wear suits. I was wearing a plain dress of crinkly cotton. I didn't think the dress was plain until I saw Seth all dressed up. He hadn't told me where we were going, but from the looks of him it wasn't a plain place.

We both said hi while I closed the door behind me. We went down my front walk, just as we had the Saturday before. That Saturday night seemed long ago. So much had happened since then.

We were at his car. It was a long, silver bullet, and it had thick carpeting and a roof that slid back to let the sunshine or the stars in and a stereo AM/FM radio and cassette player with a digital display and a bunch of other features. Seth must be rich!

"Nice car you've got here," I said.

Was I glad he hadn't seen the inside of my house—his car was more of a home than my house! I bet he lived in a mansion.

"Thanks," he said as he started the motor. "And now we're off to what I hope will be a great evening. I made reservations at a place that was highly recommended, okay?"

Why was he asking if it were okay? He had already done it. What if I said no? But it sounded nice—highly recommended and all.

He said, "The reason I said highly recommended is that if it's a bomb, don't blame me." He laughed.

I laughed too. On Saturday nights you're supposed to laugh. I figured out that he was a planner. I didn't know that about him before, but I didn't know much of anything about him, except school-type stuff. When we were out with Peter and Tracy, Seth wasn't in charge of anything. He was just part of a preplanned evening. But now, tonight, he was the head person.

"Where are we going?" I asked. "Where's this highly recommended place?"

Suddenly I knew the answer before he told me. I just knew it!

"Gregory's Galley," he answered. "Peter had high praise for their food and their comedy show. He took Tracy there once."

"I know."

We were going to *Mitch's* place. It belonged to Mitch and me. But what could I say? I said, "Good choice."

When we got to the restaurant, the parking lot was almost full. Not a nice way to treat a silver bullet. It could get nicked maneuvering around. But Seth glided the car around like an expert.

We went inside.

My luck, we got the same waiter Mitch and I had had. This time he wasn't wearing jeans and track shoes. He was wearing an outfit that in some small towns could probably get him arrested.

"Peter recommended the chicken cooked with grapes," Seth said when we were handed our menus.

"Okay, fine."

After the waiter took our orders, Seth said, "Well, you've been queen for a week. How does it feel?"

"Interesting. Very interesting."

"Are you getting mobbed by your royal subjects?"

"Some of them."

"Your speech was an inspiration. Ever think about concentrating in that area when you get to college? Communications, that sort of thing?"

"College? I'm not going."

Seth looked puzzled. He ran his fingers through his sandy-colored hair. But it stayed just the same: unruffled.

His hair was doing better than he was. He seemed kind of stirred up. "I thought you were going to the University of Arizona."

"You've got me confused with someone else. Plenty of kids are going on to the U. of A., so it's a natural mistake. Is that where you're going?"

"No."

He looked embarrassed.

"Actually," he said, "I'm going to Harvard."

"Good choice."

That's what I had said about going to Gregory's Galley. Harvard deserved something better. But I was a little put off. Seth seemed just too surprised that I wasn't going to college.

And he wasn't finished. "Any particular reason why you're not going to college?"

"Yeah. My marks. I'm not interested in college. I want to go to work. That covers it."

*Maybe* my marks wouldn't have stood in the way. My mother's help with my homework pushed some of my marks way up at the same time that some of my other marks were coming down. My marks were always passing each other, going in opposite directions. But I didn't want to talk about college any more. Maybe Seth's evening was already spoiled. Did he only date college types? Whatever happened to last Saturday night's admiration?

He said, "Are you looking for a particular type of job?"

Good. We were through with college. We were out into the world.

"Yeah," I said, "doing artwork. I'd like to get into advertising in a department store."

He smiled. "A career woman."

He was dressing things up, as he did for his body. Nice clothes, nice words. He could date a future career woman but not a future just-plain-worker?

"I might end up washing dishes somewhere," I said. "Like, for example, in a restaurant. Like here."

He laughed.

"No kidding," I said. "What if none of the department stores wants me?"

"Then you'd have to go back to school. Art school, for training."

This guy was a real believer in education.

The waiter came back to say that they were out of grapes, but would we like to try the dinner special?

"What is it?" I asked.

Sorry I asked.

The waiter was all prepared with this long, complicated pitch about the dinner special. By the time he finished describing it, I forgot what he said in the beginning. But Seth and I both nodded that we'd try it.

The comedy show started before our meal was served. Some of the jokes were kind of nasty. A few of them were off-color. I watched to see which ones Seth would laugh at. You can tell something about a person that way.

No luck. He laughed at all of them.

I didn't.

The dinner special was better than its press release. I didn't know what it was, but that was okay.

Seth looked at me closely while we ate. He was interested. He never once got a faraway look in his eyes, the look that means he's thinking about something or someone else, or he's bored or wishing the night was over.

But how did I feel about him? Definitely an attraction there. That hadn't changed from last Saturday night. It just got *interrupted* by Mitch. Seth seemed a little older than Mitch, although they were both seniors. Maybe it was the way he dressed or his attitude. And now *he* was interrupting my feelings about Mitch. But he wasn't making them smaller. My feelings for Mitch were very, very strong. It didn't seem fair that I now had the confusion of two boyfriends when I had no boyfriend for three and a half years or so, except for a while there was Chuck-Who-Didn't-Count.

Still, who says that either Seth or Mitch would last? There was the Rona business with Mitch and the college business with Seth. When Seth was in kindergarten, he probably knew he was going on to college. And he knew his wife would go to college, too, even if she, at that moment, was occupied with sand piles and building blocks. I wondered if it were hard for Seth to get accepted at Harvard. Did he have to sweat out the waiting period? Probably not. He must have good stuff in his head or in the bank or a string of Harvard relatives or all of the above. His great-great-grandfather probably graduated from Harvard.

I decided that I never wanted to meet his family, crusty with tradition and dripping with emblems and stuff. They probably owned more blazers than a blazer factory.

Maybe Seth just wasn't my type and Mitch was. But tonight Mitch was out with Rona. That didn't make him completely my type. It made him more of a question mark. Rona—cool, powerful, and sure of herself—might slick Mitch right back into being her exclusive property.

"Shall we go?" Seth asked.

"Go?"

He smiled. "They're going to kick us out, we've been here so long."

I couldn't believe it. The show was over, the dinner was over; everything had just flown by.

When we were back in his silver bullet, gliding along, I said, "Your family's big on college, right?"

"Big? Well, they're pleased that I'm going to Harvard."

"And if a person doesn't go to college, that person doesn't have much of a mind? They have a mind maybe like elevator music?"

*"Elevator music?"*

"Yeah, elevator music. See, elevator music knows its boundaries. It exists at a certain level, doesn't go higher, doesn't go lower. It's not supposed to surprise you or challenge you."

"That's a new one on me, but it's not bad. In fact, I rather like it. I rather like you too. What are you doing next Saturday night? Since you seem kind of interested in my family, how'd you like to come for dinner?"

In a pit of well-educated alligators?

Seth was driving, looking straight ahead. How did I get into this? He thought I *wanted* to meet his family! Or maybe, happy thought, he was proud of me and wanted his family to meet *me*.

I didn't know what I was doing next Saturday night. I hadn't thought that far ahead. What if Mitch wanted to take me out?

I said, "Could I let you know in a couple of days?"

"About Saturday night or about coming to dinner Saturday night?"

He was separating the two. That made it harder for me. He wanted to tie up Saturday night. Now.

What could I say? He was too smart to believe some wishy-washy excuse. But I didn't want to say no, and I didn't want to say yes. Not yet.

I said, "I might be dead Saturday night!"

"*What?*"

"I've been getting these threatening notes."

"*Why?*"

"Don't know."

"What do the police say about them?"

"Don't know. Haven't been to the police."

"Why not?"

He was still looking straight ahead, concentrating on his driving.

"Well, for one thing, these notes might just be a prank or something."

"You mean they're not life-threatening?"

"Well, one said, 'Don't do it. You'll be sorry.' And the second said, 'You really will be sorry.'"

"What don't they want you to do?"

"I'm not sure. When you get notes like those, you can think of lots of things. Like if *you* got one, it could mean don't go to Harvard."

Seth laughed. "It probably *is* just a prank. It's somebody's idea of fun because you're queen. Forget it."

He reached up and pressed a button. The roof opened. "Let's have a little night air," he said. "And let's get back to my question. How about next Saturday night?"

This guy didn't take dead for an answer, so what else was left?

"Yes."

Besides, I really liked him. A lot.

**17**

"**D**id he kiss you good night?"

Brenda was sitting on my bed when I got home from my date with Seth.

"None of your business. But yes."

"How many times?"

"Five hundred."

"C'mon, tell me. I'm your sister."

"More than once. Less than five hundred. What are you doing up so late, anyway?"

"Are you kidding? The Sweatband Couple was working out in the gym with another couple most of the night. What kind of social activity is that, anyhow, inviting another couple over on a Saturday night to work out in a gym? They were blasting their aerobics music. I ask you, how can a ten-year-old get her beauty sleep with adults carrying on like that?"

Brenda calls our parents the Sweatband Couple, among other things.

"But what are you doing in my room? You're not supposed to come in here when I'm not home, remember?"

"Your room is farther away from the aerobics blast, so I've been hanging out here. But I didn't mess anything up. I was exceptionally neat when I opened your drawer and borrowed a pair of shorts."

"What?"

"That's why I came in. To borrow these shorts. And I found the atmosphere very peaceful, so I stayed." Brenda pointed to a pair of my shorts beside her on my bed. "I need these for early tomorrow morning to play tennis. Mine are all in the hamper."

"You mean you opened my drawer and took out something that belongs to me?"

"That about sums it up. Look, I wouldn't have done it if I wasn't desperate. Your shorts are too big for me. By the way, how come you're hiding letters in drawers? I saw two envelopes addressed to you. Typed. Do boys type love letters these days? That's tacky."

I glared at Brenda. I had just come in and hadn't even taken the shoes off my hot feet. And here she was, in charge of my room. "Brenda, did you read my mail?"

If she'd read those notes, she'd know they weren't love letters. But I had to make sure.

"Of course I didn't read your mail. I've got my standards. I don't read other people's mail. So tell me what was inside."

Brenda stretched out on my bed. She was so anxious to butt into my business.

"I hate to disappoint you," I said, "but—"

"No, you don't hate to disappoint me. You hope to disappoint me. Let's be honest here."

"Okay. Well, here's your disappointment. Those aren't love letters. Now *leave!*"

"So what are they that you've hidden them under your shorts?"

"Brenda, you'll have a wonderful time imagining what they are if I don't tell you. So I'm going to rob you of your wonderful time. They're just prank notes . . . probably."

She sat up. "Probably prank notes?"

I went to my bureau, opened a drawer, grabbed the two envelopes, and tossed them on the bed.

"Here, read these and leave."

Brenda eagerly opened both envelopes and took out both notes. Then she read them. "These are in chronological order," she said. "You didn't tell me that. You have to read Note One before Note Two."

"Okay, you've read them. Now go to bed."

Brenda didn't move. "This is hairy stuff," she said.

"Hairy? I told Seth about them tonight, and he said they were probably just a prank. I told Mitch about them, too, and he just approached the whole thing scientifically. But no sweat in either case. It's probably just a big nothing."

"Are you kidding?" Brenda carefully put the notes back into their envelopes. She handed them to me. "These notes were either written in friendship or in hatred. I'd go with hatred."

"Why?"

"You've got two sororities that want you, two guys who are going after you, you're queen of the school. There's a lot of hatred possibilities there. For everybody who loves a winner, there are five who, well, I'm talking trouble here."

Brenda folded her legs under her. "Boy, you've become such an interesting sister all of a sudden."

I studied Brenda. For some crazy reason I respected her opinion. She wasn't talking hot air, she was talking human behavior. And she had just enough meanness in her to recognize it in somebody else. But who? Who was sending these notes?

"Okay, you're so smart, what do I do?" I asked.

"Be suspicious of everybody."

"Everybody?"

"Sure."

"But if you don't trust your friends—"

"You live longer."

"Brenda, you're going too far. You're saying that somebody in The Pack—"

"Or the entire Pack as a group—"

"Okay, you're saying that *she* or *they* are warning me not to join Chi Kappa?"

Brenda nodded. "Or the note could mean the opposite—don't do what you're doing now, which is staying in The Pack."

"I never thought of that. It could be from Chi Kappa Sorority or somebody in it, trying to get me away from The Pack?"

"Yep." Brenda got up. "That's it for tonight. I haven't even gone into the possibilities that the notes are about Mitch or Seth. I'm booked up for the rest of the weekend, but if you'd like to make an appointment with me to discuss this further, perhaps sometime in the middle of next week—"

"*Leave*, Brenda. I'm not kidding. Go!"

She left, taking my pair of shorts with her, of course.

I sat down on my bed. Sometimes it's okay to get advice from someone who's older than you, more experienced, and wise. But to have to take it from a ten-year-old brat who goes into your bureau drawer without asking, who sits on your bed all smug and satisfied that she knows more than you'll ever know, it tells you that you've got a long way to go in this world.

18

**S**unday night I went to the meeting of The Pack. It was held at Holly Wood's house.

When I walked in, I felt like a member *and* I felt like an outsider. I felt like two people, and one of them was there to spy.

I sat down on the sofa. Tracy came in almost immediately and sat down beside me. I should have offered her a ride to the meeting.

She grabbed my hand. "I was out with Peter last night," she said, "and he told me that Seth is wild about you."

"No kidding. If Seth told that to Peter . . . I mean, do guys confide stuff like that? Anyway, Seth asked me to have dinner at his house next Saturday night. Like, his parents are going to be there."

"His house? You're going? I hear they're very rich, and they act that way too."

"Maybe I should have said no."

Tracy squeezed my arm. "Don't worry about it. This is just terrific."

She was so friendly, she had to be on my side. She would never have written those notes to me.

But how about the other girls?

"Tracy, did you tell any of the other Pack members about Rona's inviting me into Chi Kappa?"

"C'mon, Fritzi, I wouldn't dignify that so-called invitation by repeating it."

But how could I be sure that she hadn't said anything? How could I be sure they *all* didn't know?

Elissa called the meeting to order. She started to talk about Pack business. My mind wandered. My eyes wandered. I looked around the room at my sorority sisters. They were also my friends, weren't they? What does it take to turn you against a friend? How strong is a friendship if you can blast it to bits with suspicions? Is it only as strong as the good times, which means it's also as weak as the good times? Fritzi Melvina Tass, who can you *trust*? I envied Kim and Elissa. They had been through a lot together. They had something strong and wonderful going. I figured that Tracy and I were close too.

But Brenda had planted distrust in me. She'd brainwashed me, that's what she'd done.

"Now *everybody* pay attention!"

Elissa had raised her voice. I was the temporary treasurer of this group, I had responsibility. Some responsibility. The Pack was more interested in collecting members than money. But I paid attention.

Elissa was all revved up. "We have news! We have merchandise! We have our outstanding Jacket Committee,

Bridget Jawinski and Marlene Garcia. Remember those names, girls. They will go far in the world of . . . jackets! Marlene?"

Marlene was sitting on the floor next to a huge paper bag. She pulled something out of the bag. She said, "I have here, in person, for all of you, our Pack jackets!"

She held up a jacket, spreading out the sleeves. The jacket was bright red nylon, really bright. Then Marlene turned the jacket around so that we could see the back of it. She was looking right at me.

"Fritzi," she said, "this might be of some small interest to you." She held the jacket higher. "But I really think it will be of *tremendous* interest to you. Just look at how *pow* your logo turned out! A big hand, ladies, for our logo designer extraordinaire!"

There was the logo I had designed for the jacket! THE PACK was written out with a big swirl of white letters slanting across the back.

Tracy clapped. The other girls joined in.

But I didn't feel good. I felt awful. I could wring Brenda's neck for making me distrust these girls.

Marlene wasn't finished. "Nobody can miss that our colors are red and white, and nobody can miss 'The Pack' on our backs. Let's all wear our jackets to school tomorrow. You can see they're lightweight, and if the nylon feels a little sticky, well, what's perfect in this world? So now I dig into my big bag of goodies."

Marlene started to hand out jackets. "We had to settle for one-size-fits-all, so let's hope it does."

"Oh, well, a minor detail." Stephanie laughed.

Everybody laughed. Even me.

Marlene handed me a jacket. I stood up and put it on. I

wished I had a mirror so I could see my logo on the back of me. But I saw it on the other girls. My logo, my Pack.

It was confession time. "Hey, everybody," I said. "Fritzi here with a news bulletin."

"You're having a meeting in your house *finally?*" Holly asked.

"What?"

"Next meeting, Fritzi?" Elissa looked hopeful. She wasn't going to let this big chance go by. Finally a meeting at the Tass house. Maybe.

I was trapped.

"Okay," I said, "but it might have to be in our gym because, uh—"

"Your gym? Neato!" Deena said. "We haven't had a meeting in a gym yet."

"Settled," Elissa said. "And thank you for that news bulletin, Fritzi."

"No, that wasn't it," I said. "What I've got to tell you, and it's like don't-faint time, is that Chi Kappa invited me to become a member!"

It was don't-faint time. Everyone except Tracy looked really shocked. They *couldn't* have known; they *couldn't* have gotten together and written those notes!

There we were, dressed in our Pack jackets, attending Shock Theater together.

Elissa said, "This is incredible. Are you *sure*, Fritzi?"

"Sure I'm sure. Like, Rona Dunne, she's been bugging me. She even hinted that she'd help me find a job."

Tracy was laughing. "Oh, Elissa, it's just some kind of joke. You know Chi Kappa."

"Yes, I know Chi Kappa," Elissa said, "and that's why I don't think this is a joke."

"Yeah, Rona even invited me to a meeting. They're not supposed to do that unless you're actually a member. But she said she was so sure I'd want to join after I shared this experience that she was making me this offer."

Bridget spoke up. "It's all so simple. We've got the queen and Chi Kappa wants her. It's clear to me. So, Fritzi, how are you going to handle this?"

Tracy was quick to answer for me. "She's going to forget it," she said. "That's what she's going to do. Would you like me to type up a nasty little turndown note for you, Fritzi?"

She said "type up"! She said "note"! Tracy typed everything. She had a typewriter at home. She had a typewriter at school. She hardly knew the meaning of handwriting. That's what happens when you get to be a newspaper editor.

"Uh, no thanks, I'll handle it. I mean, it might even be interesting to go to a Chi Kappa meeting."

I looked at the faces around the room. "Don't you girls think so?"

Kim made a face. She said, "If you want to go as an individual, Fritzi, well, that's up to you. But if you want to show up at a Chi Kappa meeting as a member of The Pack, I think we all should vote on that."

Elissa nodded. "What do you say, Fritzi? The Pack is a democracy. We don't force members to do things. So is Kim's idea okay with you?"

Now I was the one making a face. "It might be okay if I understood it. Like, the same body—mine—would show up whether I'm just a person or a member of The Pack."

"I know what Fritzi means," Stephanie said. "We don't have to vote."

"I disagree," Deena said. "I think we should vote."

This was turning into a debate. Maybe I should tell them about the notes. Give them the whole picture. But Brenda would say "wait." She didn't trust anybody.

Kim sighed. "This is getting out of hand. Fritzi will just use her conscience about going to the meeting."

"My *conscience*? I mean, that can be a revolting word, Kim. You're telling me I shouldn't go."

"Well, they're not your friends, Fritzi. That's really all I'm trying to say. And if you turn your back on your real friends—"

"I wouldn't do that! Never!"

"Girls, girls," Elissa said. "Whatever happened to our jacket euphoria? Let's not spoil it. We've got to get on with the meeting. Fritzi will simply do whatever she thinks best."

I clammed up. The invitation to join Chi Kappa was most likely canceled by now, anyway. Mitch had probably told Rona about us. But it was like Frantic City when I told The Pack about the invitation. Maybe they thought I was a deserter or a traitor or something.

Sometimes I think life loves me, and sometimes I think life hates me.

**19**

"**S**tay away from Mitch."

These were the words that greeted me when I got home from the meeting of The Pack, heard the phone ring, and answered it.

The phone call was, of course, from Rona.

She had plenty to say. "Now, Fritzi, that's not a command or anything, but it's a firm suggestion that I'm giving you as a friend and future sorority sister."

*She still wanted me in her sorority?*

She went smoothly along. "I'm sorry to have opened so bluntly, but I'm really speaking as a *friend.* Sometimes friends have to be blunt. You see, Mitch and I have been going steady for a long time. But I realize you already know that. What you probably don't know is that unfortunately he's got a bit of a roving eye, and you're the sixth or seventh girl his eye has . . ."

"Roved to?" I offered.

"Something like that. Now, I'm sure he's very sincere about what he tells you, but next week or next month he'll be very sincere about what he says to another girl."

"I don't get this, Rona. If he keeps looking at other girls, why do you stick with him?"

"Because he loves *me*. He always comes back to me. In fact, nobody even realizes that he's *strayed* because his interest in other girls is so fleeting. Just a few weeks at most, and on the sly, of course."

Mitch had been seeing me on the sly. But he must have told that to Rona, and she was making it up that he did it with other girls too. What had Mitch told me? That he hadn't even looked at another girl since Rona and he started dating. Not until I came into his life.

Rona was probably reloading her gun with more ammunition. I waited for the next shot.

Here it was. But she had changed angles. She said, "I saw you at the spring prom with this absolutely gorgeous hunk, and he seemed so devoted to you. You wouldn't want to lose him, would you?"

Was this a threat? Would she try to ruin me with Seth by telling him about Mitch? I had a right to date both of them.

She was still moving along. "Well, I think I've covered everything, but I will add that we missed you at our meeting tonight. May we expect you at our next one?"

"Yes, you may expect me," I said.

I knew that I had to go to that Chi Kappa meeting the next Sunday night. I had things to clean up, things to find out, things to sort out. Probably Chi Kappa was too smart for me and I wouldn't learn anything. But how could I let the chance slip by?

Was Rona licking her chops at the other end of the telephone wire? She sounded happy. "Very wise decision, Fritzi. The Baron house at seven next Sunday evening. Will you need a ride or are you taking your car?"

"I'll take my car."

"Okay. I really enjoyed our conversation, Fritzi."

"I know."

And that was it. We hung up.

I felt as if I were being kicked around. Rona was telling me what to do about Mitch. The Pack was pushing me and pulling me or something. And Brenda was helping me and kicking me at the same time. And whoever wrote those notes was definitely trying to control me.

Could anything that Rona said about Mitch be true? Was there a small, ever so small, almost-invisible-to-the-naked-eye chance that she was being honest in warning me about Mitch? Would he dump me after he dated me a few times?

No. Fish fudge.

Fish fudge. Fish fudge. Fish fudge.

Rona must have gotten on the phone to her sorority sisters immediately after our conversation.

The first thing at school the next morning I ran into the Baron twins. I mean, I took one step inside the school building and there they were.

My good, close friend Tulip Baron, whom I hardly knew, crush-hugged me as she said, "You're coming to the meeting at our house! That is so super, Fritzi. You figured it out, didn't you? You have everything to gain by becoming a member of Chi Kappa. What do you owe those girls in The Pack, anyway? You won't be hanging around with them after you graduate. What you'll have instead is the honor of being able to say, 'I was a Chi Kappa girl.' "

Tulip was messing up my jacket. I bet there was a big crease across where it said "THE PACK" on the back.

Daisy looked puzzled. "You're really quitting The Pack, Fritzi?"

"Hey, hold on there. I didn't say I was quitting The Pack. I simply said I was going to a meeting of Chi Kappa."

"Chi Kappa is giving you the big rush, Fritzi," Daisy said. "They're very good at that."

Did she mean that as a compliment or a putdown?

Tulip released my body. "Time for class," she said. She started to walk off. "Oh," she called, "I guess you'll be donating that jacket to Goodwill or the Salvation Army."

Daisy quietly caught up with her sister. They disappeared down the hall.

I brushed myself off. I was brushing off the memory of Tulip Baron.

"Hey, girl with the jacket!"

It was Mitch, coming toward me, grinning, eager, handsome. I saw ready to be crush-hugged again, but he didn't touch me. He looked me over. I turned around so he could see the back of me. "I designed the logo," I said. I couldn't remember if I had told him about the logo before. It was easy to brag about.

"Nice job, Fritzi. Where can we show it off this Saturday night?"

"Huh?"

"I'm asking you out, and why don't you wear this jacket?"

"This Saturday night? I'm going to somebody's house for dinner. But Friday night I'm free."

"Are your parents dragging you somewhere for dinner Saturday? It sounds deadly. Can you get out of it?"

"No, and it's not exactly my parents."

"Look, I told Rona about us. She took it very well. Hard to figure. Anyway, didn't you notice I'm asking for the big date night, Saturday? We can go anywhere you want. I thought you'd be happy. Everything's out in the open now."

"I am happy. It's just that Seth already asked me to eat with his family and, anyway, we can go out the *next* Saturday night, can't we?"

Mitch looked hurt.

"What is this?" he asked. "A rotation system? Seth has you one Saturday night, I have you the next?"

"But you're still going to date Rona, aren't you? That's what you told me."

Mitch shrugged. "I honestly don't know. I'm beginning to think she was more of a habit than anything else."

"Did you ever break this habit before now?"

I was remembering what Rona had told me over the phone the night before.

Mitch gave me a careful look. "Odd question. The answer is a big no. But I already told you that. And, believe me, I was prepared to feel like a rat when I told Rona about you. But she was so calm."

No wonder. She figured she'd get him back by getting rid of me. But I didn't tell him.

I said, "The whole dating system is unfair, anyway. If you stop having feelings for someone, you're a rat. It's like you're not *allowed* to do that."

"Good point. We should be allowed. Fritzi, *you* should. It's your right. I'm stepping back. Go out with

Seth, get to know him, give him a chance. If it doesn't work out, I'll be around. But clear your head. Think of us as history."

"No. You don't get it. My feelings for you haven't *changed*."

"Fritzi, they haven't even developed. And they won't with your rotation system. I wasn't being sarcastic when I called it that. I almost fell into the same trap myself."

Mitch looked at his watch. "I have to go to class. We'll talk again. Really."

I watched him go. What he said made sense, but if he were so smart, why had he fallen under Rona's spell in the first place? Still, love isn't a brains situation.

Rona had fed me a line of bull about Mitch. She wasted her breath. We split up without any help from her. Would he go back to her now?

I took off my jacket and folded it into my backpack. At lunch I was supposed to put it on again. The Pack members had decided that we should all wear our new jackets at our table. I wanted to be by myself for lunch. I wasn't in the mood for any group activity. My mind was too full of Mitch. But I couldn't let the other members down.

I did well in my classes that morning. And I got a good mark on a homework paper I had written myself. My mood picked up.

I was one of the first Pack members to get to the table at lunch. Only Stephanie was there earlier. Then along came Deena. Here we were, slowly filling up, a red-and-white display. Elissa and Kim marched in together. The smiles on their faces! This was such a moment for them. They had started The Pack from nothing. Just a dream. The dream of the outsiders. But now, as I looked over at

Chi Kappa's table, Buckingham Palace looked positively anemic. Most of the members were there, but so what? The splendor, the glory, belonged to The Pack. Were we finally more powerful? Had the shift really happened? If so, exactly what had brought it off? Some yards of red nylon and some bunches of white felt? Is that the way power works? I guess so.

If you look as if you've got it, you've got it.

The third note arrived on Saturday.

I was the one who found it in my mailbox. Nobody else was home. I had heard the mail truck go by, so I went outside even though I dreaded opening the mailbox. All the mail was hot, but I was used to that. Half the year out here in Palm Canyon, everything arrives baked.

I couldn't stand opening that envelope. I knew there was another note inside. I could tell by the way the envelope looked. What if I just tossed it, dumped it unopened into the wastebasket? I couldn't, I couldn't!

Do everything fast, Fritzi. Get it over with. I ripped open the envelope and pulled out the note. I read it.

"THINK SLOWLY AND YOU'LL KNOW THAT CHI KAPPA SORORITY IS NOT FOR YOU."

There it was, the motive revealed. The letter writer had gotten bolder. Don't join Chi Kappa!

All sorts of suspects disappeared in my head. I was left with one. Tracy.

She must be on a new kick. Writing anonymous letters. Her hair used to be purple and pink-orange and green, but now it was natural brown. Maybe she needed a new weird outlet. But still, this anonymous stuff didn't fit her personality. It was a shrinking-back way of communicating, and Tracy didn't shrink.

Maybe she thought I wouldn't listen to her if she tried to give me advice. Tracy believed in the power of the typewriter, and here it was.

But I was mad at her for scaring me. A person doesn't have a right to do that to another person.

I went back into the house.

Call Tracy. Be calm. Be cool. Keep the friendship. It's worth saving. But tell that previously purple-haired person to butt out of my business. I can make up my own mind about my own life.

I picked up the telephone.

"Another note?"

Brenda was standing there.

"You scared me," I said.

"Didn't you see me follow you into the house? I was coming down the street when you got the mail. So what does today's charmer say?"

"It says 'None of your business.' "

"I figured you'd get one like that."

"You'll keep bugging me about it, won't you, if I don't tell you what's in it?"

"Actually, no. Kids my age, we just flit from one interest to another. Your notes, well, that was last week. Or was it the week before? The memory dims."

Brenda started to leave the room. She turned back and said, "How can I not let you share your anguish with me? What kind of sister am I, anyway? Just toss me the note and I'll give you my opinion."

I tossed her the note because I wanted her opinion. It was that simple. I knew who sent the note, I knew why it was sent, but maybe she'd have something to add or subtract.

The note landed on the floor. Brenda picked it up. She read it while she picked it up.

And she had something to add. Praise for herself.

"I was right," she said. "I had two basic theories, and this supports one of them, that the notes came from a member or members of The Pack to warn you not to join Chi Kappa. What are you going to do about it?"

"I'll take care of it."

"Be strong," she said. "Now, what's to eat? I'm hungry."

Brenda looked in the refrigerator. "Oooooh, a brownie. There's one brownie left. May I have it, pretty please?"

Sometimes she was still only ten years old.

"It's yours," I said.

I took the note to my room. I decided not to call Tracy. This wasn't a telephone thing. It was nose-to-nose confrontation. And this wasn't the day for it. I was going out in a few hours. I had to get ready. I had to be in an up mood. I was going to the Berns house, mansion, palace, whatever, for dinner.

The note took away one fear. At least there wasn't somebody out there trying to scare me away from Seth.

Correction.

I hadn't met his family yet.

# 22

"**M**ay I take your jacket?"

I was at the Berns' palace, and Mr. Berns was reaching for my Pack jacket. My jacket, my identity that I had planned to wear through dinner. Mr. Berns was smashingly dressed in a green blazer and gray pants. Mrs. Berns was also smashingly dressed in a silky baby-blue outfit. They both looked as if they had just gotten off a yacht.

And here I was in my red nylon Pack jacket over a canary-yellow cotton sweater and matching yellow pants. I looked as if I just got off a rowboat.

I had taken Brenda's fashion advice: "If you look like you tried too hard, they'll *dismantle* you, they'll take you apart."

I surrendered my jacket. Something that works in a cafeteria sure can fizzle in a million-dollar house, which is

99

what this looked like. I didn't know what Seth's parents did for a living, but they must have either done it very well or very dishonestly.

"Drinks are on the patio," Mr. Berns said after the maid had taken my jacket from him.

We all walked out to the patio. There was an Olympic-size pool out there, and plants and flowers and a fountain, all very snazzy. But there was a real scene-stealer. Many scene-stealers. Statues. About a dozen of them, and they were of people and they didn't have any clothes on. I think those are the most expensive kinds of statues.

The drinks had already been placed on a chrome-and-glass table that had four matching chairs around it. The drinks were different kinds of fruit punch in matching pitchers. The pitchers and glasses matched the table and chairs. Manic matching gives me the creeps.

We all sat down and sipped. Mr. and Mrs. Berns were staring at canary-yellow me. I didn't know what to say.

They did.

Mrs. Berns started off. "Are you a native of Palm Canyon?"

"Oh, no," I said. "I come from New Jersey. And, boy, sometimes I miss it so much. Like, I hate to look at a map of the United States because then I see how far I am from New Jersey."

Mrs. Berns nodded.

I went on. "I still have friends and relatives back there, and sometimes I remember their coming into my house, huddled against the cold and bundled up and breathing hard, kind of pink and frosty, and I know that I might never see that again."

"That's a fascinating thing to miss," said Mr. Berns.

Seth was smiling in a pleased sort of way.

"Well, listen," I said, "people are the most important thing a person can miss."

Mrs. Berns gave me a strange look.

I explained. "Even if you don't come from New Jersey, even if you've lived in the same place all your life, some of the people you once knew are dead. And if you really, really think about it, most of the interesting people are dead because there are many more dead people than live people, so it's only logical."

Mr. and Mrs. Berns and Seth were fidgeting in their chairs.

"Sorry," I said. "I didn't mean to talk about death. I mean, you have a very lovely home here, and we can talk about that. Those statues are, like, from a museum."

I was doing better. Mrs. Berns asked, "Do you go to museums often?"

Seth got into the act. "Fritzi's an artist."

Now we were on the right track. Mr. and Mrs. Berns leaned closer to me, as if they were accepting me, like they were going to pat me, a stray dog they had decided to keep.

I was waiting for artistic-type questions to be thrown at me. But everyone turned quiet and we just kept sitting and sipping. It surely was beautiful out there by the pool and the naked statues.

It wasn't until we were in the house and in the middle of dinner that Mrs. Berns got going. "I've always admired artistic people," she said.

I shrugged. "Admiration happened to me when I drew something for the school newspaper, and I loved it. But, think about it, what's to admire? If you're born with a tal-

ent, no credit to you, right? If you're born with brains, no
credit to you. If you're born with beauty, no credit to you.
But, see, it's okay to praise brains and talent, but it's shal-
low to praise beauty. And yet they're all in the same 'born
with' category, right?"

Mr. and Mrs. Berns looked extremely puzzled.

I was getting wound up. It was enthusiasm time for me.
I felt like talking.

And so I just kept going. "High school life is an example
of admiration gone wild. Unchecked. Untamed. Your
social success is often based on your looks. But even if
you're ugly, you can shine in the classroom where you
have a chance of scoring various brain victories. So there
are different types of admiration victories available in
high school. I'm not in the winner's corner with my looks
and brains, but I got lucky with my talent. Lucky. And
before I graduate I'm going to do another drawing for the
school newspaper."

"That's interesting," Mr. Berns said as he cut his steak. I
think it was steak we were eating. It looked like it, but it
didn't taste like it. We also had tiny potatoes and vegeta-
bles in a cream sauce.

Seth was really close-mouthed. He must have had a
plan for his folks and me to get acquainted, and he was
just sitting and watching and eating his food.

It was hard to tell how things were going because when
people have a lot of money and a lot of surface manners,
they don't let you know what they're really thinking. If
Mr. Berns were wearing a tank top and had earthy mus-
cles and sweat on his forehead and dirty fingernails, I'd
get his drift pretty fast. I mean, he would have *told* me
already. Same thing with Mrs. Berns. Flaking nail polish,

a dress with a bunch of cents-off coupons stuck in a pocket, a fatso figure, and I wouldn't have to wonder about anything.

"Before you graduate?" Mrs. Berns said.

"Huh?"

"You were saying that you were going to do another drawing for the school newspaper before you graduate. I imagine that's an arena you'll be exploring in college too."

"Oh, I'm not doing any exploring in college. I'm not going."

I pierced a potato. This was heavy news to unload on Seth's upper-class parents.

Mr. Berns was potato piercing too. "My wife and I didn't go to college," he said.

"*What?*"

"My husband said that we didn't go to college." Mrs. Berns was smiling.

"I don't get it," I said.

"What don't you get, Fritzi?" Mr. Berns asked.

Seth looked cringy. No wonder. What was I *doing?* His parents weren't shook up over my education. I was shook up over theirs.

"What Fritzi means," Seth said quickly, "is that she knows I'm going to Harvard, and it's fairly obvious that we have a lot of material advantages here, and so she naturally made the assumption that we're a college-oriented family."

I usually can't stand it when people explain what *I* mean, but in this case Seth did fine.

"My wife and I were fresh out of high school and dirt poor when we got married," Mr. Berns said.

I relaxed. He was getting a tank-top personality.

"We were fortunate in that we had a friend who lent us money to buy a little variety store," Mrs. Berns explained.

Mr. Berns took up the story. "We slaved day and night in that store," he said.

"And you made a big success of it," I said, finishing the story for him.

Mr. Berns laughed. "On the contrary. The store was a failure. But it was in a part of Palm Canyon that was eventually taken over by developers. They paid us a substantial sum of money just to get the land that the store was on. Then Mrs. Berns and I invested our money wisely —"

"Very wisely," Seth added.

"So you had dirty fingernails when you started?" I said. "I like that. I like that a lot."

Now I knew why Seth had invited me to meet his parents. He knew it would work out.

But he had another reason too.

# 23

We were sitting in Seth's car in front of my house.

"My parents are crazy about you," he said.

"How can you know?"

"I can tell."

"It's very unusual for a guy, a teenager, to invite a girl to meet his parents. Like, it's usually None of Your Business City between a guy and his folks."

"True. But I have no intention of hiding you."

Seth put his arm around me. "Fritzi, what I said about my parents being crazy about you, it applies to me too."

With his free hand Seth pulled something out of his jacket pocket. He held it up so that it caught a thin stream of light coming into the car. It was a tiny pin with a face or something on it.

"This pin was in my parents' store," he said. "Part of the

merchandise. It has very little monetary value but considerable sentimental value. It's one of the few items from the store that they've kept. They've given it to me. I want you to have it. I want you to—how do I put it?—go steady with me, date me exclusively."

I drew in my breath. I didn't expect anything this heavy, this *definite*.

"You're going away in the fall," I said.

"That's months and months away. And I'm not skipping the country. Well?"

I thought about Mitch. If I said yes to Seth, I'd be saying no to Mitch. Why wasn't one of them a rat? It would have been the easy way out for me. I would have learned something gross about one or the other that would have eliminated that one. Maybe I would in time. I didn't know either of them that well. But my Fritzi Tass instinct told me that they were both good guys.

I needed time. Not to find out if one of these guys were a rat but to find out how I really felt about them.

"Seth," I said. And I stopped him as he was about to kiss me. "I'm, like, overwhelmed by this. And honored. You have to know how *honored* I feel. But, see, it's too much of a decision for me to make right now. It used to be that nobody expected much of me. I was sort of left alone. But now I've got more stuff coming at me than I can handle. Two sororities, two —" I stopped myself.

"Guys?" he finished. "Mitch Brenner, your king. He's my competition, isn't he?"

"Yeah. How did you know?"

"I observed him at the prom. When you were crowned queen, when you gave your speech. Are you dating him?"

"I was, in a way. It got sticky."

This was awful. Mitch had backed away because of
Seth. Now what if Seth backed away because of Mitch?
Instead of fighting over me, they'd be retreating over me.

"Seth . . ."

"Don't say anything else, Fritzi. Here, I want you to
have the pin. Go out with whomever you want, but keep
going out with me too. That's all I ask."

"That's all?"

"That's it."

"You're what I would call an understanding guy."

"Some people might call me a jerk."

"Not me," I said.

I took his pin. I stuck it on my favorite piece of clothing.
My Pack jacket.

"I'm supposed to do that," he said.

I took the pin off.

"Your turn," I said.

He restuck the pin.

I leaned over and kissed him.

Then I said "Your turn" again.

24

"**M**ay I speak to Mitch, please?"

Fortunately it was still early in the evening. I mean, quarter past ten on a Saturday night isn't terribly late to make a phone call.

"I'm sorry. He's out for the evening."

A woman with a nice voice had answered the phone at Mitch's house.

She asked, "Would you like to leave a message?"

Is he out with Rona? That's the question I wanted to ask. But I didn't. I said, "This is Rona."

Was this a slip, was this part of my investigative technique, was this a lie, what was it? I was *thinking* that he was out with Rona. The thought worked its way through my brain and this is what came out.

108

"Rona?" she said. "You're not Rona. Young lady, whoever you are, is this your idea of a joke?"

"No. This is Fritzi Tass, and I didn't mean to say Rona. I
mean, I don't think I meant to say Rona. Doesn't your
tongue ever slip?"

"Oh, you're the *queen!* Why didn't you say so? Mitch is
at the auto show with his father. I don't expect him back
for another hour or so. Would you like Mitch to call you?"

"Well, I'm going to bed. Tomorrow will be okay. Or if
he doesn't call, I'll see him in school."

"I'll tell him you phoned. And I'm sorry if I was a bit
short-tempered."

My royalty bought me an apology.

"That's okay. Good night."

I hung up. So Mitch was out with his *father.* Not Rona.
Good. But I had to talk to him. This was such a confusing
time of life.

But Seth wasn't confused. He was something else.
Patient. He was fighting for me by being patient.

I looked down at the pin he had given me. I was still
wearing my jacket. I took off the jacket so I could see the
pin better. It was an inexpensive, novelty-type pin; you
could tell. But it was a dear, funny little pin with a gremlin
face on it.

It made me feel romantic.

I took the pin off my jacket and pinned it on my nightshirt and hoped I wouldn't stick myself on it when I slept.

**M**itch didn't call Sunday morning. Mitch didn't call Sunday afternoon. And now it was time for me to leave the house and go to the Chi Kappa meeting.

I had told his mother that if he didn't call, I'd see him in school. So that must be what he planned to do: see me in school.

*Who are you kidding, Fritzi? He should have called.*

Tomorrow could be a very big day at school. Yelling and screaming at Tracy, yelling and screaming at Mitch. Project, projects.

The best way to get your mind off something nasty is to think of something more nasty.

The Chi Kappa meeting.

I put on my Pack jacket and drove off.

There were quite a few cars parked in front of and near the Baron house when I got there. I parked across the street.

I got out of my car, crossed the street, and went up to the front door. I was at the mystery house, the very private house of the Barons. My house is kind of private, too, but that's because it's so dumpy inside.

Daisy and Tulip answered the door together. They looked alike and different, as usual. Daisy was the one without the make-up, and Tulip was the one all fixed up. They looked like Before and After, but I thought that Before looked better.

"Hello, hello," Tulip said with a big red-glossed smile.

Daisy didn't say one word.

Two hellos, two people. I guess it evened out. But Daisy did not seem happy to see me.

I didn't have a chance to think about that because suddenly the other Chi Kappa girls were all over me, mobbing me.

"You came!" Melanie Deborah Kane squealed. "You came to our meeting! You're a survivor."

"Don't you want to dump that jacket?" Allie Grendler asked.

Here I was, walking into a Chi Kappa meeting wearing my Pack jacket. Talk about nerve. I had pinned Seth's pin back on it. I now had a collection of little holes from the pin.

"Who's your tailor, Fritzi?" Selena Vonder asked in her sour, screechy voice.

"Now, now, Fritzi is our guest, our future member,"

Rona said. "Concentrate on the essentials, girls. However, Fritzi, if you'd like to dispose of—deposit—your jacket, the bedrooms are on the next level. Just toss it on any bed up there."

"I . . . okay."

Why make a fuss over something so small? So I'd take my jacket off. Besides, this was a chance for me to look around the Baron house. I was a little curious as to why the Barons were so private.

I went up to the second level where the bedrooms were. I walked into one of them. It was a big room, and I immediately noticed that there was a picture of daisies in a field on one wall. There were also daisies, real or fake, in a couple of vases.

This had to be Daisy's room.

Tulip probably had a room with a tulip theme. I felt jealous of kids who had houses that were taken care of enough to have themes. I had given up on my bedroom because the theme seemed to be cracked plaster. Daisy's room was decorated in yellow, green, and white. There were a lot of pictures of her and Tulip on a wall and on top of her dresser, and there was even one on her desk between a typewriter and a pile of schoolbooks.

I had an urge to see Tulip's room.

I started down the hall. But Carrie Reis grabbed my arm and practically yanked my jacket off me. "We're *waiting* for you, Fritzi."

They were saving a seat for me. On the sofa. Fritzi Tass wasn't going to be seated on the floor like some of the other girls.

Rona called the meeting to order. "Girls, tonight we have a new member—*perhaps*—so let's all be on our very best behavior. And by the end of the evening maybe we'll have turned that *perhaps* into a positive commitment. A yes!"

Why was Rona so anxious to have me in the sorority? She couldn't actually like me, not with the Mitch situation.

I took my seat and the meeting began. What was the sorority going to discuss tonight? News, clues; I was waiting for anything that came my way. I was here, finally, at a meeting of Chi Kappa Sorority. I felt as if it were going to my head. This was secret stuff!

It wasn't secret stuff. I should have known they were too clever to talk about confidential things in front of me. They talked about raising their dues, they talked about starting their meetings half an hour earlier, they talked about having fewer refreshments because so many of the members were on diets. This was the stuff sleeping pills are made of.

But if Tracy could see me here, she wouldn't think this was sleeping-pill stuff. She'd just die. I had ignored her notes, but I wasn't going to ignore them tomorrow. At school tomorrow I would have it out with her.

Why was I thinking about that again? I should be paying attention here. Maybe I could still pick up something of interest.

Of interest? Rona was saying, "So it's decided. We'll be starting our meetings half an hour earlier from now on. Everyone agreed?"

"I don't agree," Daisy said. "We could do things faster, and then we wouldn't have to start earlier. I've noticed at our meetings that we get going very slowly, like snails. Slowly is fine if you have something you really want to think about but —"

Crystal Jameson interrupted. "Daisy, listen, some of us have dates after the meetings, and we have school the next day, and I say we go with the earlier starting time."

Daisy shrugged. "Whatever you say."

"Decided," Rona said.

Suddenly she turned and looked straight at me.

"And what have you decided, Fritzi?"

"About what?"

As if I didn't know.

"Fritzi, really. We don't want to pressure you but the time has come. You can't put it off any longer."

"Believe it," Tulip said.

The mood of the meeting had changed. This was the real business of it. Me.

I had thought I was so smart coming here. Fritzi Tass, investigator. But there was nothing to investigate. The Chi Kappa girls had planned a nothing meeting in my honor. No way were they going to let me in on any of their secrets unless I became a member.

I didn't want them. Boy, I didn't want them! I knew that long before I came. But being with them made me not want them even more.

"I'm not joining," I said. "I'm a member of The Pack forever."

"The Pack?" Carrie Reis sneered. "You mean the sorority that tries harder?"

Most of the Chi Kappa girls were laughing.

"Oh, Carrie, they have to try harder," Selena screeched, "to keep up with us."

The girls kept laughing.

I stood up. "We could have passed you a long time ago,

Selena," I said. "Except that, like, we don't want to go in your direction. *Ever.*"

I was surrounded by frozen faces.

"You had your nerve coming here," Allie Grendler said, "if you weren't going to join!"

"Correct," I said. "I had my nerve. And what's wrong with nerve? Like, let's hear it for nerve."

I didn't hear anything.

Daisy stood up and tapped me lightly on the shoulder. "Want your jacket?" she asked politely.

She didn't seem mad. She just seemed to think I should leave.

I agreed.

Daisy got my jacket before I could. She walked me to the door. She didn't say anything else. Neither did I.

I left my first and only meeting of Chi Kappa Sorority.

26

**B**renda was sitting on my bed when I got home.

"You expected me to be sitting here, didn't you?" she asked. "So tell me everything."

"I didn't join."

"Well, of course you didn't join. But what happened there? Did you find out anything?"

"Nope. They had it all well planned. They didn't spill any secrets."

"How devastatingly boring."

"I told them off."

"How devastatingly unboring. Good for you. And now what?"

"Now what *what?*"

"What are you going to do about the person or persons in The Pack writing you those notes?"

"Brenda, I'm taking care of it tomorrow. Don't bug me so much."

"But how are you taking care of it? Which one? Which ones?"

"Brenda . . ."

"Okay, okay. Anyway, I think you handled all of this very well. Caught between two worlds, two sororities, two boys. Oh, by the way, one of them called."

"Who?"

I knew the answer. Seth was checking in. I was just about to transfer his pin to my nightshirt, getting ready to spend another night with it.

"Mitch," Brenda said.

"Mitch?"

"Yeah."

"Why didn't you say so?"

"I just did."

"I mean, right away. As soon as I came in."

"Then I'd never find out what went on at the meeting."

Brenda got up from the bed. "You want me to leave so you can call him in private. I'm leaving. But I just want to say, and I can't say this *enough,* I love your life, Fritzi. I love it, I love it, I love it. To go from virtually *nothing* to all of this—"

"Brenda, I can't say this enough. *Out!*"

"If you decide on one, may I have the other?"

I closed the door behind her.

I dialed Mitch's number.

He answered.

"It's Fritzi returning your call, which was a return call in the first place."

"Hi, Fritzi."

"Hi."

I was looking at Seth's pin. "Here's why I called, Mitch. I've been thinking about what you told me at school. About what you call the rotation system's being a trap. And about your stepping back so I can go out with Seth."

"And?"

"And, well, it makes sense. *But*—if you step back too far and for too long, Seth's gonna get me. See, if you don't take me out at all, I'll never get to know how I feel long-term about you. So I think this rotation system is okay as long as it's honest. Like, you have to rotate honestly. Openly. You'll know that I'll also be dating Seth, and I'll know that you're going out with Rona . . ."

"Who says I'm taking her out again?"

"Who says you're not? See, that's another thing. You don't really know yet."

Mitch didn't answer.

"Think about what I said. And remember, we're still king and queen of Palm Canyon High. Let's be more than figureheads. Let's do something that counts. Okay?"

"Sure."

"You mean it?"

"I mean it."

I didn't have anything more to say.

Mitch did.

"Bring your lunch tomorrow," he said, "and we'll eat outside and talk some more."

"You mean it?"

"You just asked me that."

"But it wasn't about food. Look, I'll bring the sandwiches. I'll pack two brown bags. And I'll surprise you with their contents. I just hope you like spinach sandwiches."

He laughed. "See you tomorrow. And remember, I'm a big eater."

We said good-bye. I hung up.

Settled! It was settled that my love life was unsettled.

27

It was asking too much of my body to fall asleep—
after that Chi Kappa meeting, after my conversation
with Mitch, and before my confrontation with Tracy
tomorrow.

Tracy. I had to concentrate on Tracy. What would I say
to her? "You don't send notes like that to a friend"? "You
should have had faith in me that I'd never join Chi
Kappa"? "If you don't know that about Fritzi Tass, you
don't know anything"?

I got up, turned on the light, and took the notes out of
my drawer. I looked at the latest. "THINK SLOWLY
AND YOU'LL KNOW THAT CHI KAPPA SORORITY
IS NOT FOR YOU."

*Think slowly.*

That was kind of a strange way of putting it. But teen-agers are good at talking weird. I might even be the champ that way. But, listen, if you can't be you, who else can you be? Anyway, "think slowly" wasn't really weird. Didn't Daisy Baron say tonight that Chi Kappa's meetings got going very slowly, like snails? She said that slowly is fine if you have something you really want to think about.

*Slowly is fine if you have something you really want to think about!*

"Think slowly," the note warned.

No, it couldn't be. It couldn't be Daisy Baron.

There was something else. Far back in my mind. *C'mon, Fritzi, what was it?*

It was that day I gave Daisy a ride home from school. When I was trying to get information out of her about Chi Kappa. But she had changed the subject. We were in front of her house and Daisy had thanked me for the ride and then out of the blue she said, "Think slowly."

I didn't get it then.

I get it.

I get everything.

It wasn't Tracy who wrote those notes, it was Daisy Baron! Daisy, who wasn't sophisticated, investigatively speaking. She didn't know that a favorite expression can trip you up, an expression so favorite and close to you that you don't know you're using it.

And she almost got away with it. If I hadn't gone to the meeting, I never would have tied everything together.

Wait till I tell Brenda. Brenda, who knew it all. Of all her guesses about who wrote those notes, she never even considered that it might be a member of *Chi Kappa* warn-

ing me not to join Chi Kappa. Little Miss Know-It-All,
your big sister knows more.

But another big question had to be answered: Why did
Daisy send those notes? She didn't want me in Chi
Kappa, that was as clear as a scream. But why did she care
that much?

I set my alarm to go off at five o'clock. Maybe I'd sleep
till then, maybe I wouldn't. But I had to get up early. I
had to get to school early. I had to stake out my position
and wait there. I had to be finished with this note business, once and for all.

28

"**D**aisy!"

I called out to her.

Daisy and Tulip were getting out of their car in the school parking lot. I had been waiting in mine.

They both stopped and looked around, trying to see who was yelling.

I got out of my car and rushed up to them.

Tulip said, "Fritzi, don't be so hyper. If it's about what you said at the meeting last night, I think we all agree that you're just not Chi Kappa material. Chi Kappa doesn't hold a grudge. You're forgiven."

"You're too generous," I said. "Like, it's to upchuck how generous you are. But I came over to talk to Daisy. In private."

"Anything you have to say to Daisy can be said in front of me."

"No, it can't," I said. "Daisy's entitled to privacy. Who are you, her keeper?"

Tulip tugged at Daisy. "C'mon, Daisy."

"No!"

"No? You want to stay here and talk to Fritzi? The girl who insulted our sorority under our very roof?"

"Yes," Daisy said.

Tulip shook her head and walked away.

Daisy leaned against her car. She was waiting, her soft green eyes staring at me behind her glasses, her dark hair blowing in the early-morning breeze.

I opened my backpack. I took out the three notes and held them up.

"Why?" I asked.

Was she going to deny that she wrote them?

No. It came pouring out. "I had to do something. But I couldn't just tell you to your face. I couldn't go that far. I *am* a member of Chi Kappa, after all."

"Tell me what, Daisy?"

She turned away. "You found out I did it. Can't we just skip the rest? Now that I know you won't be joining Chi Kappa, can we forget it? I'm sorry about the notes. Maybe you'll forgive me? I was thinking that they might sound a little scary if you didn't know who wrote them and what was behind them. But it's all over now."

"*Not* all over, Daisy. You owe me an explanation."

"How did you find out it was I?"

"Your 'slowly' expression."

"Oh."

She was thinking about that.

"Maybe I wanted to be found out," she said. "I'm not sure."

"Let's get back to the explanation you owe me."

"But I feel as if I'm not being loyal to my sister. She was part of it."

"Of what?"

I was in the pulling-teeth business, no doubt about it.

"Of Chi Kappa's strategy."

"I'm waiting."

Daisy sighed. "Okay, Chi Kappa lost two members during this school year. Kim Adler and Tracy McVane. And now Kim and Tracy belong to The Pack. What's even worse is that Kim became one of the founders of The Pack. Chi Kappa's rival. So the girls of Chi Kappa hatched this plan to try to lure a member of The Pack away to join Chi Kappa. Just think what a victory that would have been for Chi Kappa. And what a defeat it would have been for The Pack!"

"But why did they pick me?"

Daisy hesitated again. "You're not going to like some of this, but here it is. You've got prestige being spring queen. That part's okay. You know that Chi Kappa's high on prestige, so this angle is pretty obvious. But don't be too flattered. They also thought you'd be the easiest Pack member to win over, and since you're a senior and there's not much time left in the school year, you wouldn't be around very long."

"This is like a sleaze plan!"

"Yes, and I kept telling Tulip that it wasn't the right thing to do. But she said there's a war going on between Chi Kappa and The Pack and that this came under the rules of war. I told the other Chi Kappa girls how I felt, too, but they didn't care. So then I had the problem, should I tell you? I just couldn't do it face-to-face, so I wrote the notes. I couldn't write everything in the notes, so I thought if I just kind of warned you . . ."

Daisy's voice trailed off. Then it picked up. "I couldn't use my own handwriting, so I typed the notes."

"I saw a typewriter in your room last night. But I never dreamed—"

"Did the notes scare you? I didn't mean them that way."

"They scared me. And I was about to pin the blame for writing them on someone else."

"I should have told you. I should have had the courage. But Tulip—the sorority means so much to Tulip."

"How about you?"

"Well, Tulip and I stick together. And now I'll have to tell her what I did."

"Why? You don't have to."

"Yes, I do. I'm sharing this with you, so I have to share it with Tulip."

"But you *don't!* I've got a sister. I don't share everything with her."

"Well, I just have to now."

What a relationship they had! This was spooky. Daisy wasn't her own person. Everybody knew she was part of a package deal, but can't a package ever get split?

Daisy had a faraway look. "I hope Tulip doesn't tell the other members what I did."

"She wouldn't do *that*."

"She might."

"No, she wouldn't," I repeated. "Like, my sister is real bratty, but she would never go that far."

"We're going to be late for class," Daisy said abruptly.

She ran off.

I just stood there.

I was glad I never told The Pack about the notes. Tracy would never know that she had taken on the role of chief suspect in my life. But wait till I tell The Pack about the fireworks at the meeting last night. Wait till I tell them what I said. They'll be glad I went. Well, maybe not glad, but not disappointed, either.

But what Daisy told me, that was a secret. I couldn't tell anyone in The Pack. I'd be revealing Daisy if I did that.

Chi Kappa never wanted me. They were just trying to use me. Funny thing, that didn't hurt my ego. My ego was finally a safe thing.

I walked into the school building. I saw Daisy trying to catch up to her sister. Daisy was so eager to demolish herself. What was going to happen between them? Would Daisy get kicked out of Chi Kappa?

I felt sorry for Daisy. I felt sympathy for this person who had scared the life out of me. But she had taken a risk for me. And I owed her. I owed the person who wrote me scary, anonymous notes.

Sometimes I think life is just one big switch.

"Fritzi!"

Elissa was down the hall, calling to me and rushing toward me at the same time.

She was wearing her Pack jacket, and I thought about how the members of The Pack were a continuing walking, running, sitting advertisement for our sorority.

When Elissa reached me, she put her hand on my shoulder. "Fritzi, my girl, the word's out about what you said at the Chi Kappa meeting last night."

"It is? Who told you?"

"Kim told me. Bridget told Kim. Holly told Bridget. I

don't know where Holly heard it. It's come a long way, the information."

"Things were much simpler when Tracy was in Chi Kappa. She and her mother were good sources of material about what was going on. You could depend on the source. None of this chain stuff."

"Well, it doesn't matter where the information came from, Fritzi. It only matters that you stood up for The Pack."

"My pleasure."

"We're all looking forward to the meeting at your house."

My downfall.

But I didn't say it.

I said, "Well . . ."

"Gotta go. Nice work. See ya."

Elissa left as fast as she'd come.

I was in good standing with The Pack again. And maybe having a meeting at my house was better than worrying about having a meeting at my house. Get it over with.

I was having a very strange day so far. My confrontation with Daisy, Elissa's hit-and-run approval, and a lunch with Mitch to look forward to. Or dread.

What if it turned into a good-bye lunch?

**29**

**S**itting outside on a wall under the Arizona sun with two sandwiches, two pieces of fruit, four cookies, and Mitch Brenner as a wall-mate is about as high as a girl can rise popularity-wise at Palm Canyon High. It doesn't have the pizazz of going to the prom, but it says that you've picked out a private place within the crowd. It says that you're willing, and maybe eager, to have yourselves on display as a pair.

But popularity wasn't on my mind as we sat and ate our sandwiches. Something called the future was on my mind.

But Mitch said calmly, "Nice day."

I answered, "Yeah, isn't it?"

And he said, "Yeah," and I was thinking that if our English teachers were around we'd get zero for self-expression.

We were a few minutes into our fruit and cookies before I finally said, "About our telephone conversation . . ."

He kept eating.

I repeated, "About our telephone conversation . . ."

Then he repeated, "About our telephone conversation . . ."

"Ha ha," I said. "Not funny. Don't you want to talk about it? You didn't like the lunch I packed and you're making me pay for it."

"The lunch is fine, you're fine, and the telephone conversation was fine. But I'm hungry and I'm wolfing the food down. I can't wolf and talk."

I was too anxious. But it was too late to back off and not be anxious.

I waited until he was ready to talk.

He finished the last cookie. Then he said, "About our telephone conversation . . ."

I couldn't help it. I laughed and so did he. But I cut my laughter short. I had to know what he was going to say before he said it. Why couldn't I read his mind?

He went on. "I more or less agree with what you said on the phone. I have some reservations. But on the whole . . ."

"On the whole, what?"

"On the whole, what are you doing Saturday night?"

"You're asking me out? You're in such a joking mood . . . is this a joke?"

"No joke. I'm asking you out. I accept the fact that I'm not the only guy in your life. I accept the existence of Seth

Berns. But he'd better watch out. He's got competition."

Mitch reached into his pocket.

"Look what was in my cereal box this morning," he said. "I don't think it was intended for my age group, but what the heck."

Mitch held up a tiny plastic figure of a soldier.

I didn't get it. He had just asked me for a date, and I hardly had time to let that sink in when he pulled out this cereal-box soldier.

I decided I had a right to look stupefied.

"You see this fellow, this little green fellow?" he asked.

I nodded.

"This fellow was trying to tell me something at breakfast. He doesn't look articulate? He looks like the quiet type?"

I nodded again.

"You have to look beyond the green plastic. This little guy is saying that it's okay to fight for something you want. I'm not talking guns or bayonets. I'm talking about not quitting."

"But maybe you had already made up your mind, and this soldier, well, what if you had eaten another brand of cereal?"

"This fellow was an affirmation rather than an inspiration? You may have a point there, Fritzi, but we'll never be sure, will we?"

Mitch pressed the soldier into my hand. "He's yours," he said. "From me. To remind you that I'm not giving up. So, how about Saturday night?"

"Yes! The answer's yes."

I clutched the hot little soldier.

I don't like military things, but this soldier, with his

stern green face and silly stiff body, had risen from the cornflakes or whatever with precision timing.

"Thanks, Mitch," I said.

"Just what you always wanted?"

He laughed.

But maybe it was.

**30**

**A**fter school I started on my homework right away. I closed the door to my room to try to keep Brenda out. Not that a closed door was an obstacle to Brenda, but at least it was a hint.

It felt good to be in control of my homework again. I could do it. Sometimes badly, sometimes beautifully. But at least *I* was doing it and not my mother. She missed the job, I could tell. But she wasn't the one trying to get an education. She already had one. Two, she didn't need.

I heard a knock at my door. Brenda? Would she do anything as civilized as knocking?

"Come in," I said.

It was my mother.

"Sorry to interrupt you," she said.

"That's okay. But I don't need any help with my homework."

"It's not your homework, it's your home that I've been thinking about. It's time that I got started with the redecorating. What do you think of blue and tan as a color scheme?"

"I like it, but is this for real?"

"Yes. I know I've been a little slow in getting to it."

"The Pack is bugging me to meet over here. In fact, they're planning on it. The gym looks okay. But the falling plaster in the rest of the house . . . I mean, these are my friends, and none of them has falling plaster."

"I'm sorry. I'm really getting cracking on this project."

"When?"

"Any day now."

"What does that mean?"

"Maybe tomorrow. Well, I'll let you get back to your homework. Need a little help?"

"No. Thanks. I've got it under control."

"Okay."

My mother turned to leave.

"You did say maybe tomorrow?" I asked.

"Yes."

She left.

Would my mother's tomorrow ever come? Probably not. Someday, when I got married, I'd get myself a house that was perfect. Mitch and I? Seth and I? I wouldn't mind sharing falling plaster with either of them. I wouldn't care where I lived.

The telephone rang.

I picked up the receiver.

"Hello."

"Fritzi?"

"Who else?"

"It's Seth, Fritzi."

"I know. Hi, Seth."

"Hi. Are you taking good care of my pin?"

"Your pin's in good condition in intensive care. I'm looking at it right now. It's on my Pack jacket, and my jacket's draped over a chair. Your pin's in fine shape, I guarantee it. This is one happy gremlin."

Seth laughed. "Okay, Doc."

"Is that why you called?"

"No. I called to ask you for a date, of course."

"Of course."

"Saturday night?"

"This Saturday night?"

"No, Saturday night a year from now. Problems?"

"Not exactly. Like, it's not a problem, but . . ."

"Oh, I get it. Another date. With Mitch."

"He asked me a few hours ago and I said yes."

"I should have asked you when I gave you the pin, but I was dealing with broader issues, you might say."

"Yeah, our entire absolute relationship and the future, and so what's one Saturday night when you're dealing with stuff like that?"

"Are you trying to console me? If you are, here's the best way. Break the date with Mitch."

"Oh, I couldn't do that unless I got sick or something, and then I couldn't go out with you, anyway."

"Forget I even brought it up. He got there first and that's that. But I'm going to grab you for the next Saturday night. How about it?"

"Sounds great."

"Be thinking about what you'd like to do and where you'd like to go. Whatever you do this Saturday night, we'll do something better the next one."

This was competition, all right! Things were heating up. And, oh, how I loved that fire.

Seth wasn't finished. "I'm going to be faster than Mitch from now on."

Maybe I'd be booked weeks and weeks in advance.

I asked him a question, half-serious, half-joking. "Saturday night a year from now, the one you mentioned, should I hold that open?"

"No. By then I'll have won out over the competition."

"You're Mr. Confidence."

"Maybe you'll be Mrs. Confidence."

What did *that* mean? Don't ask. It's just too heavy right now.

"Well, Fritzi, I'll let you get back to intensive care. I'll call you soon and we'll decide on our big Saturday night. Come up with something original. You're good at that."

"Okay."

We said good-bye.

I sat and stared into space.

The school year was closing down soon, but my life was opening up more and more. So much had happened this year. Royalty, admiration, fear, acceptance, and now, with two guys after me, a little Crowd Control might be needed.

But who's complaining? I switched from being the girl nobody noticed to the girl everybody's noticing. I feel as if I'm on top of the world, and the view's not bad up here. Not bad at all. But I almost blew it by getting too close to Chi Kappa Sorority. Going to their meeting was risky business. I'm a Pack person. It's in my genes; it's on my back.

And those notes warning me not to join Chi Kappa almost cost me my sanity. But that's over too. I'm glad it was just Daisy who wrote them, and not a dangerous, depraved individual.

I finally learned the difference between depraved and deprived.

I finally deprived my mother of doing my homework.

I've learned a lot this year. I found out what it's like to be in the middle instead of on the sidelines where I used to be. But listen, there's something to be said for the sidelines. It's peaceful.

But I wouldn't go back. Now I'm Queen Fritzi, courted by Seth, courted by Mitch, and it's great, to say nothing of amazing. I can be friends with both of them. I worked it out.

Brenda said she loved my life. I love it too.

I looked at Seth's gremlin pin on my jacket. Then I looked at Mitch's little soldier which I had put on my desk.

I picked up the soldier and took it over to my jacket. I held the soldier in front of the gremlin, facing it.

"Square off, you guys," I said, "and come out fighting."

*About the Author*

---

MARJORIE SHARMAT is one of the most popular and prolific authors of best-selling books for today's young readers. Her more than eighty books, published in thirteen languages, have sold over twelve million copies. Among her novels for young adults are *Square Pegs*, *I Saw Him First*, *How to Meet a Gorgeous Guy*, *How to Meet a Gorgeous Girl*, and *How to Have a Gorgeous Wedding* (also available in Laurel-Leaf editions). Her most recent novels were *He Noticed I'm Alive . . . and Other Hopeful Signs* and its companion volume, *Two Guys Noticed Me . . . and Other Miracles*. Marjorie Sharmat lives in Tucson, Arizona.